The Reality Pirate's Guide to the Astral World and Dreams

ZOLI ALTHEA BROWNE

D.Div, PhD, D.S.M., PhD

ISBN: 979-8-9902437-1-2 (Hardcover)

Contents

Introduction to the Astral Realm

When you dream, you go to the astral realm. It is a frequency, or a place of being that is very real, but it is not physical. And it is an exact replica of this physical world. That's why they say as above, so below. The astral room itself is non-definable. It just is. You can't point to it and say this is where it is. But it surrounds us, and there are different levels of it.

Like anything else, the higher up you go in it, the better it's going be. It is a place where illusion happens very quickly. The beings in the astral realm can believe that they're Napoleon, and nobody's going to tell them they're not. Then, somebody might start channeling them and say they're channeling Napoleon.

That's why you have to be very careful. There's a case in the first book about a woman who had beings surround her overnight who said they were all seraphim angels and told her that she was one, too. And that's just garbage because you're not. So, that person now lives their life believing this is who they are, and they're lying to other people. It's a cult. The astral realm is fraught with all kind of garbage, but it also has great beauty.

There are great writings and communication that come from the upper levels of the astral realm. But I think the most important thing is, it's a state of being rather than a place of being.

The astral realm is not a common word unless you are in Theosophy or New Age belief systems. It's more like it's a TV show where things just happen and you pick up on it. I don't think people believe they have much control over the so-called astral realm. You certainly have control over yourself and the physical, and there are ways of controlling your dreams or your wanderings in the astral realm. It takes some effort and some work.

It's mainly an unconscious situation for the masses of humanity and why would they know about it? We come here to deal with this physical world, and there's nothing wrong with doing it. If you see a chair, you want it to stay a chair. You don't want it to turn into an eagle. But in the astral realm, whatever you think, that's what happens. You become whatever you're thinking.

I don't understand all of it. All I can do is intellectually talk about it. People do meet up in the astral realm. The Monroe Institute does a lot of work in the middle areas of the astral realm. In the first Reality Pirate book, I wrote about how you can meet up with others in the astral realm and do some good. Many of the beings that we think are angels that appear in our dreams, are dreaming humans or deceased astral inhabitants taking on a role because we are that loved. Most of the so-called angels are Masters, again, because we are that loved.

Angels started popping up in Church doctrine only in the late first century CE. Before then, there was little mention of them.

Angels don't appear to people. That might be a contentious point, but they just don't. We just keep hearing they do because they have wings, but wings are a Devic thing, not necessarily an angel, though you would think it was.

We encounter other people while dreaming, and when we are helping them, it is a beautiful thing. We are responsible for our actions in dreams as we are in our awake life. But are we actually guides for other people?

It depends on who you are and what you're doing. As above, so below. Whatever you're doing on the Earth plane, you're probably doing that same kind of work in the astral realms. And vice versa. And there are people that go into their dream body and their astral body and do help other people in that way. I would refer people to the Monroe Institute for those courses and the ways of doing that.

As above, so below. Whatever you're doing on the Earth plane, you're probably doing that same kind of work in the astral realms.

So, it has to be intentional. With intention comes consciousness, and with consciousness comes intention. And that's always the preferred method, but most of us just wander around out there wondering what the heck happened. It's like we're characters in a play that somebody else wrote.

My husband can change his dreams when he goes into them. If he doesn't like it, he'll change it. But most people have to go to the

Monroe Institute or somewhere here and spend days, hours, weeks, years, whatever, learning to do that, but he just does it. It's not a skill that I have. He says he learned it from a monk in Thailand when Thom would take folks around the Buddhist wats (temples) and instruct them on the culture. Thom spent years in Thailand in his Special Forces 1st Group deployments. We all have things that come easily to us like that.

In these pages, you will find stories and lessons from my experiences so as to uncover and explore the nature of dreams and the astral world. Throughout the book, there are sections where some of your questions are answered. If you have others, please get in touch.

Reading this book may awaken a dream world with which you are unfamiliar, or you may notice an increase in dream activity. It is a heightened awareness of the astral world that unleashes those dreams. May we all find a smoother transition between dreams, the astral realms, and what we call the here and now.

The whole concept of reality pirate is a state of being, not a person to strive to be like. Everyone should just be themselves, stay grounded in the physical world, and then come back. Because reality is not what it used to be, it can be helpful to seek the wisdom of change. The Reality Pirate concept is a way to explore other ways of being. RP has experiences which we delve into in other books.

All things of this physical reality world have a beginning, a middle, and an end. Whereas in the astral world and dreams, things are not always what they seem. As always, my prayer for you is to keep trying and to find your way through this world and the next. Go forth into the world of dreams with an understanding that it is all connected to your purpose.

Your Questions Answered: When did the Reality Pirate (RP) come to be?

When I first moved to Olympia in 1985, there was a spiritual group in Yelm Washington that put out a newsletter called *Windwords*. They came out to interview me, and it was quite hysterical because they knew I was working with the Zeta Reticuli. I was just off-the-chart weird.

They couldn't even print what I said. It was so scattered because connecting with some of these energies that I could rarely find the exact words to communicate with others. I was getting great stuff, but was challenged with channeling it. I wasn't grounded.

So, the Reality Pirate started in the early 1990s when I collaborated with a man who could read my scribbled writings, and I think we had a sacred contract that we would do that. He would put it into a cohesive form and then we would have it printed before sending it out in a newsletter.

My point in doing the Reality Pirate newsletter was to do what these off-worlder beings asked, which was to get this information out there to the population of folks who could use it and need a confirmation of their own experiences. It's like sitting next to somebody at a dinner, and they don't speak English, and you don't speak their language. But when we speak the same languages when we're in the same energy field, I think we can help each other in that way. And I don't believe that my work or anybody's work is for everybody. So, take what resonates.

By always keeping the price so low on things related to RP, I have a better chance of helping more people.

What's funny about RP, my alter personality, is he's the part of me that can go and do and say about anything he wants, and he can't get caught. He'll just dematerialize and go somewhere else. There is no photograph of RP because he's a shape-shifter. He can't hold form very long in 3D planets.

When RP's emotions change, he has trouble shifting. His whole purpose is to not get caught. He is a Gemini, and he is able to express the inappropriateness of many things, which is wonderful.

It is akin to being with your kids and they're five and seven years old. You act silly. They encourage you to embrace that part of yourself. Then, if you go to a board meeting, you're going to act differently. At least you will if you don't want strange looks.

When I was living in Texas, I remember hearing this story about a man who took his wife to a company dinner. She was talking, and in the middle of dinner, people stopped talking, and they started staring at her. She was cutting the guy's meat next to her from his plate like he was four because she didn't get out much. We've all done goofy shit like that, but we have to be appropriate. We're afraid of showing these other pieces inappropriately, and that's a very strong urge in all of us.

As we get older, many of our beliefs will change, and we find ourselves not wanting to do some things that we've done before and wanting to do other things. And there's nothing wrong with that if it's appropriate for each of our own lives. RP reminds us to shift our lives accordingly.

zoliartexoticamontana.com/music

For Every Child

The Nature of Dreams

All channeling comes from the astral realms. That is where you connect with your third seal or chakra. When we leave our physical body and dream, that's the world we enter. During my years at my farm in Washington State, I was trained to receive such intel through the third chakra. I had not yet learned to raise my consciousness to the heart and above. This was the normal educational process demonstrated in my wandering around the astral world of illusions and beauty.

I hope you're not disappointed. I'm not going to tell you what your own dreams mean because I don't know you. I'm not much on the dream books anyway. Your own interpretations are something for you to discern. But what are they? Why do we dream? Are they the real world? I plan on answering none of these questions. I respect your brilliant ability to discern the images of your own dreams. What I will do, however, is tell you about several very strange dreams which have stuck with me over the years.

They aren't all bad; they're just confusing. I bet my dreams are similar to yours. Lots of images present potential for various interpretations. Most of my dreams present this way. I guess I'm not that interested in consistent dream journaling, but I do write down the cool ones.

So, what do you think? Are dreams astral realm experiences, or are they images produced by the physical brain? Truly, I don't know. When I was a kid, I had awful night terrors, sleepwalked and often awakened screaming bloody murder. This did not endear me to bunkmates at summer camp. My dreams were fraught with icky beings and frightening, non-definable aspects of life on this earth. But I know now that I was a budding psychic medium working unprotected and uneducated. I am passionate about helping kids who are in that same energy field.

I was not yet fully protected because I was working out the usual karmic load. I chose to douse myself within this incarnation. When I was a teenager, my dreams continued to expose lower astral images, but I began to gain a measure of conscious control when I began studying psychic phenomena. I'm glad I did not know then that the schooling would take a lifetime! When I joined the Rosicrucian Order in 1976, I began a decades-long schooling which offered me solace and control over the emotional components of my dreams.

I studied Edgar Cayce's work and researched the nature of reality. Dreams appear to be yet a different reality than the consciousness of daily life. The Monroe Institute, one of my favorite neural vacation spots, offers week-long sessions on lucid dreaming. I did not attend that particular class, but I hear it's just brilliant. When I mentioned to my husband Thom that the Monroe Institute offered that class, he said, "Oh yeah, I can do that. I learned it from a Buddhist monk when I was in Thailand with First Group."

My JSOC hubby has travelled the world as a Special Forces Medic and later on as a JSOC Operator, so the dude has more talents than us normal humans. True dat. So, he taught himself to change his dreams if he doesn't like them. Me, never. But here's a fun thing. Twice in my life, I experienced the out-of-body thingy. Both times I was riding a bicycle down the Champs-Elysees in Paris towards the Arc de Triomphe. Both times, I recall saying, "Oh, I'm having an out-of-body experience," and then I'd wake up. I was raised speaking French and later attended a summer school on the Cote D'Azur in Nice, so France is a second home to me. It makes sense that I'd find myself there during a lucid dream. Maybe we follow what we live. What do you think?

But the bicycle thing was peculiar. Was that a real dream, or what was it? And yes, tomes are written on out-of-body experiences, so look it up. I'll tell you, though, I do believe that lots of dreams are tension reliefs from stressors we have during the waking hours. I meet people and go places in some dreams, which, when recalled, do reflect the issues I'm dealing with in waking life.

> *Those crazy dreams that seem so real and unforgettable when realities merge are Ah-ha moments from our souls or from guidance.*

But what about those crazy dreams? You know what I'm talking about, the ones that seem so real and unforgettable when realities merge? I theorize that those are Ah-ha moments from the soul or from guidance. Some folks have prophetic dreams, but I don't. Mine always contain females and strong ones at that. Maybe guys dream mainly of other guys,

I don't know. So, I know you want me to tell you about some of these dreams, don't you? Well, here we go.

I guess it was thirty years ago; that would be around 1993. I dreamed I opened the front door at the farm and saw a smallish, dark-haired lady standing there. She marched inside and walked right into my bathroom, saying, "I'll have this one here." As she turned to face me, I noticed her dark, piercing eyes circled with black eyeliner like Cleopatra might've worn.

Later that day, as I walked past the kitchen window and glanced into the pasture, I saw a dog sitting with its back to me.

It turned its head, and I saw it had those exact eyes. Being the codependent rescuer personality I was at that age, I adopted her immediately and named her Chelsa. She was a total pain in the butt. She didn't get along with any other dogs and was pissy, just like that bossy lady in my dream. But lo and behold, I began to psychically hear what I assumed were Chelsea's words in my head.

Chelsea soon gained popularity through the Reality Pirate newsletter with their own section called, "Ask Chelsea."

I have no idea what was up with that, but the canine seer was frighteningly accurate. I could not make up what I heard from that dog, but here's what happened next. I had a dark, foreboding dream one night. I was in an unknown land, viewing a menacing black sky and a very large prison-like structure, totally black on barren desert-like ground. Nothing living. It was just awful. I heard a deep rumbling and I found myself standing on cold stone steps leading down into a pit inside the structure.

Chelsea was leading me, looking back to see if I was following her. We came down into a barren gray room of stone, a deep pit. There, a Lakota man in a wheelchair looked up at me and said angrily, "Go to hell!" I jolted awake only to see Chelsea staring at me from her spot next to my bed. Have you ever had anything like that happen? It's awful, just awful. But I knew that it was a Plutonian messenger leading me into a deep, dark place of learning, insisting that I go down into the pit to find the light, to courage up, and literally go to hell.

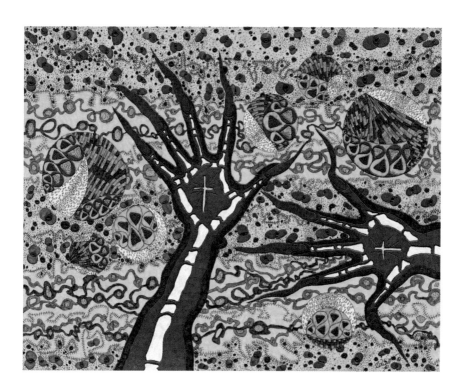

Your Questions Answered:
How do I control the bad thoughts
I have or get rid of them?

Many people think they can't control the thoughts they have. We all have bad thoughts. We need to stop watching them. The Buddhists are masters at this, I just love them. The Buddhist system looks at the act, not the thoughts.

That is actually how I quit overeating when I was binge eating out of nervousness as a teenager and into my twenties. Finally, one day, I decided I was going to quit trying to diet and quit trying to lose weight.

Instead, I just watched what happened when the thought came up. I learned that when I felt upset, I would go eat a bag of cookies. After a while, I could see the effect so, it kind of melted away. I have since learned we have to watch our thoughts and we have to detach from them.

Maitreya says (and this is an important statement) that the **greatest drug is detachment**.

When we are detached, we are still engaged in feeling, but we don't have the emotional piece. Emotions are the real killers. They land right below the heart in the gut. So, these thoughts that we have are connected to the emotions of the body.

For me, it is a racing mind. I wake up at four in the morning, and there goes the brain. It is just rattling and rattling. I stay in bed saying every prayer I can think of, every poem, every song; my heart is racing. And finally, of course, I just fall back asleep. Then I wake up in the morning thinking and wonder why that happens?

Sometimes, the more sensitive people are going to be picking up on too much disturbing shit, both internally and globally. That needs to be taken into consideration. It's not all your stuff. The more aware you are, the simpler your life is going to be, but don't think that this stuff isn't going to affect you because it will.

Does it help to not watch the news or avoid other things? Well, it depends on what kind of person you are. I've had to learn to watch the news, and detach from it, and say, well, this is the reality that is going on. Detachment doesn't mean that you don't care, but you're not trying to be emotional and to fix something that you can't fix.

It's a hard one. I don't think we ever get it. Since I've been working on these books, I'm absolutely convinced that we just never get it all done. That said, we still have to try. We are born to try! That simple effort is the blessing fueling compassion and hope.

Never quit. Love your efforts even if they sink and fall short of your goal. Keep trying. You can do this; I believe in you. The point is to try because we do chip away at it. In each life, we chip away at this stuff more and more and more. But the answer to it is meditation and service. That's what the world teacher Maitreya says. Check him out.

Go within to try to detach and then say, how can I make this world a better place? What can I do to serve others? And be honest with yourself, just being a so-called normal person living your life every day, doing your duties, caring for your parents, your children, your animals, your job; all that counts as service.

That's very important because we're getting out of ourselves, and emotion keeps us locked in ourselves. So, when we have these emotional dreams, with these emotional thoughts, we are just stuck on ourselves.

Your Questions Answered: Do we go into the astral if we are not dreaming?

Near-death experiences would be one instance of that. I think maybe people in comas are alive in the astral world consciously. The astral realm is one of the seven levels, and it is so connected to the emotional body, which is very much connected to the physical.

They interact with each other in ways that we can only imagine. I had a dream the other night that brought it to a close. I was riding a mountain bicycle, going like a bat out of hell with another girlfriend. I don't remember who she was, but I think it's somebody that I know from the dream world. And we didn't know where we were going. We came to a crossroad, and I just said, I don't know which way to go. Let's just go right.

So, we went right, and we ended up at a little store. There was a man standing outside, and I asked him which way it was to the town. And he started to tell me every reason why I couldn't do it, why I wouldn't make it, and why I wouldn't find the town. I didn't believe any of it. All I said was where is it? Tell me. It really felt like I had healed from that dream. There was me as a female, asking a male.

In the dream, that male is the authority figure. That would be masculine and not intuitive. The dream was telling my left brain, you can't do this. It reminded me of my fears. There was a second part of that dream that had the same kind of healing element in it. Of course, I didn't write it down. (Well, maybe I just did).

The point is these dream worlds evolve. We become different people in these dreams. And the people that we become in the dreams tend to act out in the physical world and what we call our world.

And the opposite is true, too. I don't think in the dream world that I healed this abandonment issue. I think it was the physical work, recovery work, twelve step work, body code, and other psychological processes to get rid of those imprints. That brings up the idea that what happens to us in the dream state leaves magnetic, electromagnetic imprints in our brain and in our consciousness.

If in a dream, you are looking at a certain product that you'd never looked at before, the next day, you are going to see that product. We do plan our next day in the dream state. And we're given options. Do you want to do this or that? Do you want to go left or right? If you do this or that, this might happen. But we don't remember all that.

The challenge of it is if we did have continuity of consciousness, we would wake up knowing what the options were during the day. Now, that would be way cool. It's possible. And the Masters say there are many people who are now gaining that continuity of consciousness. You have to have a balance in the emotional and the physical bodies. The emotional body is in the astral world. And the physical body is what we call us.

There needs to be some sort of balance. I think I'll get it, maybe by age eighty. It may be ten years from now, but I think I'll get it. Well, think how that would change life. And if I get it, then I can teach people how to do it. But right now, I just don't get it, clearly.

zoliartexoticamontana.com/music

Child of the Sun

Discerning and Learning Through Dreams

The only place we truly learn is in the dark places because we come up for air by seeking the light. It's going to hurt. Why does it hurt? We fight truth. We crave escape from grief, pain, terror and connect with the creative love only when we think we have lost it.

Here's an example of a cool dream commo from my favorite Scottish Highland cow. When I opened my front door one night, I was greeted by my black Highland Cattle cow, Lochinvore, as though it were the most natural thing in the world. I then heard her say, "Go to kola." Go to what? I had no inkling of what they meant. That next morning, I headed to our Olympia Co-Op to see if they had any kind of drink called a go-to cola. The herbalist looked at me like I was a weirdo and said,

"Do you mean the herb Gotu kola? It's for the brain." After buying a bag, I began researching herbs for bovine health. From age six up to their deaths at age twenty-six, my pet cattle were fed a diet of various herbs and medicinals. Isn't it amazing that Spirit uses living creatures to offer messages of loving support through our dreams?

Do you think that movies and theater are a dream reality? Do actors reap karma for the roles they play? Maitreya says we must pay back the karma from our dreams. If we generate hate, fear, harm, it is a karmic debt. I don't know about you but I find that just crazy. It makes sense, though, when considering that our personalities generate these dreams, and we are responsible for our choices even in the dream states. Comically, I can't control what I don't know how to control, but I can hear my master's voice urging me, just try, Zoli, try.

> *Maitreya says we must pay back the karma from our dreams. If we generate hate, fear, or harm, it is a karmic debt.*

Has anyone said to you that you were in their dream last night, or maybe they were in yours? We do share realities with other people, so perhaps that shared reality is more vibrant than it appears. That conscious dream stuff intrigues me. The Monroe Institute has a club called the Dolphin Club, where trained people work together in the astral realm to help other people.

Many of the so-called angels and guides we encounter are actually dreaming people. Isn't that cool? We can continue our service and love on other planes even as we sleep. The Monroe Institute is in Faber, Virginia. Maybe you'd like to visit our campus. Folks from all over the world attend the Gateway Session as a precursor to the other mind-bending classes, but I digress. Here's a way cool dream I had back in 2022. I call it the Dekas Azalas dream. It took place at my farm in Tenino, Washington, although I have lived in remote Montana since 2013.

I walked out into the yard under the old Douglas Fir tree next to the deck. My friend standing to my right was playing with the dogs. All felt calm and peaceful as I viewed the valley pastures and myriad of flora in the beautiful temperate rainforest of western Washington. Something caught my eye as I looked up to see a peculiar sight. Behind me, 20 feet over my head, was a female on a steampunk motorcycle. She was dressed in steampunk attire also. She circled overhead once, looking down at my startled face.

The scene quickly shifted to me standing in front of two white sheds newly built on the old garden area near the creek. They had not been there before, and they are not there to this day. This was purely in the dream. As I entered the identical sheds, I saw lots of drawers filled with crusty old reddish, rusted tools. My friend said that he thought we could use those for something. Even though the tools looked like iron that was been left in the weather for years, I saw their value.

This woman's demeanor was serious, focused, and passioned to connect with me, although I was unsure what her purpose was. Was she delivering something as it appeared? She gave me a hug, and I felt as though she was trying to press information into my mind. Her clothing was all brown, as was the bike. Everything felt ancient and looked steampunk. She had short dark hair and lightly dark skin, sort of latte colored, with blue eyes. She had a brown leather messenger's bag and brown saddlebags on the bike.

The bike rumbled like a lawnmower would. As she circled about 20 feet above me, she looked down at me looking at her, and it all just felt surreal.

I then popped back into the first scene with the steampunk gal, watching her land underneath this huge fir tree right next to the sacred large rock in the front yard. She was clearly female but presented as a neutral energy. She presented as sort of non-binary energy, rather neutral and attractive. I found that fascinating. She walked up to me and, with a piercing stare, said the words "Dekas Azalas." She seemed familiar, but I couldn't quite understand what she meant by that name. Was she telling me who she was, or was Dekas Azalas a message?

When I looked up the name Dekas Azalas, I found several things. Dekas is an angel from heaven who is near to God. What the heck does that mean? Azalas is a boy's name, Azaliah, meaning near the Lord. Azalia is a girl's name, which means God is spared.

Azaleos is dry in Greek. I have no idea what this meant. Perhaps the messenger bag held writings. It's very interesting to me that I had this dream on 2-22-22. So, what do you think? The Masters of Wisdom never ever communicate with us through channeling or mediumship. To do so would require the medium to undergo lifetimes of training and a three-year special period of intensity, usually resulting in prolonged illness.

That's why HPB was so sick. There is more written on about this in Sacred Texts so I will choose to leave it at that and present these channel stories I'm going to tell you about only as writings and clearly not from those higher beings.

Your Questioned Answered: Why don't dreams make sense?

When we think about our physical, we know what that is. We don't see this little etheric sheath that surrounds our body or an electromagnetic sheath where all the chakras are in the astral body.

If you draw a picture of your physical body, making an outline of it like you did when you were a little kid, then you draw six more outlines around the physical. There is the astral body, the mental body, the spiritual body, and so on.

We have all these different layers, and we can put our consciousness in each one of those if we really know how. In the astral world and dreams, our consciousness is just in the emotional body. And maybe, if we develop continuity of consciousness, then we have the control. But as it is now, we're just flapping in the breeze.

It is evolution. And I always say that we're just dumb. I say that with comedy because we can't seem to go any faster than we are, even though we want to.

There is a club of people who say that this will be their last life. No. It's not your last life. It's barely one of your first ones. There's so much out there. And it's going to be hard; it's supposed to be hard.

It's a sacrifice to come to earth. It's a real sacrifice. People need to take the pressure off and not feel like they're screwing up quite so much. When we're in it, we're in it.

For someone like me who's this dramatic emotional drama queen, when I'm in it, it's hard to get out of it. I'm zero to sixty. My husband says I'm like a chipmunk running around the house. It's not all bad. I'm just wired for emotion. I joke that it's one of my most endearing qualities. But that's what I'm made to be.

I'm water. I'm in motion. That's where my art, my music, my writing, it all comes from there. The astral realm feeds us all this stuff, and we beat ourselves up about it because we can't seem to control it. That's why I say we're just dumb. We just don't know that we don't know.

That's where I am right now in my evolution. I really want people that read about my world to want to go out and find out more about theirs. I think we stimulate each other, and we can live in each other's dreams and realities for a bit.

It's like watching *Harry Potter*. I love *Harry Potter*. I love *Game of Thrones*. And so, we go into these thought forms and these realities. But the more we can learn to be ourselves, when we're in that and exit that with health, the more I think that's positive. We can pirate into different realities and see what's on this side of the mist. And then we can take what we can from it, and then it expands us in one way or another.

Kids live that up to age nine. They're in it all the time. Between ages nine and fourteen, is when the shifts start to happen. And when Maitreya comes out into the open, and when we see him and the sixteen or so Masters on TV, during the DAY OF DECLARATION, the message that he gives us will be heard in our own head, in our own language, for everyone all over the world, but only after age fourteen.

Before that, we didn't have the neurology. I'm not sure exactly what it is, but we will nurture and develop that in the future. And before the age of nine happens, we will know pretty much who those people are, who they came here to be, and to direct them with this new education. They will be guided by what their soul came here to do, their point of evolution, their physical, mental, emotional, and spiritual.

It'll be quite different than what we have right now, which is one size fits all. The school systems were just horrid growing up as someone who did not fit in. I had it very, very hard. Until I got to high school, I didn't fit in. I was autistic. Nobody knew that I was a renegade or that I was a reality pirate. Kids hated me. The teachers hated me. It was a mess. They sent me to a psychiatrist starting in fourth grade. I was so weird.

And in the so-called future, they would say,

"Oh, that one's a psychic medium. She's not weird for that."

It'll be much kinder in the future. Maitreya says every day will be new, and every day will be different in the future. Gone will be the factories. All the food will be grown on the planet by the huge machines out in the fields. Everything will be mechanized. People will have time for creativity, for art, for enjoyment, for education. It will be a very, very different world.

And that's what's coming. That's why all this crap is happening. But we don't remember that. My source of reference is Theosophy. And that is from the ancient wisdom teachings. These times have been prophesied since Atlantis hundreds and thousands of years ago. It's all laid out. Everything is ordained. But we also have free will. That's a dichotomy. We don't understand it, but it's all true.

Your Questions Answered: Can dream affects reality?

They do. Of course, what you're calling reality is our waking life. Where we identify as us, dreams do affect that. The whole purpose of having this continuity of remembering what happens in our dreams every night will help that.

I don't have any dreams that are so magnificent that it's changed in my life, but I woke up this morning feeling calmer. So, there's a lot going on, and they absolutely affect our reality, and it said, and I think this is probably valid, that at night, we plan our next day. We're given options. We can choose door one, two or three. We can pick one. And it's all a dance. It just comes together, but I think they absolutely do affect this reality. And in one way, it's just kind of all one because it's happening inside of our heads.

We need to dream. And in fact, if you don't dream, you can get sick. Literally, dreaming is very, very necessary. There are people that can explain, and I don't have the knowledge to explain that, but absolutely, it's necessary.

That's why when people aren't sleeping well, they don't do well.

Our sleep cycle is about two hours. When you first go to sleep, you go into beta sleep, then alpha, then theta sleep, which is when you're dreaming. Most of the dreaming happens right on the tippy tail end of when you're in your sleep cycle. We wake up about every two hours. We may not remember it.

Lately, I have noticed I will wake up at three or four in the morning. This is a very new thing for me, but look at what's going on in the world. It's stress, and we think we can control it. But we don't want to take the time to meditate for five hours or do this or take that. So, we just kind of deal with it. For me, the dreams that I remember when I wake up like that have been more intense than any other dreams in my life.

I think it's fascinating that the Masters say that what you do in the dream state, you have karma for that in your so-called waking life here. That's a tough one. So, if I'm whacking a bunch of zombies or whatever, does that continue into my waking life? Though, I don't really have dreams like that.

Most of my dreams are where I'm in my daily life. I'm confused, trying to figure something out. Or I'm lost. I'm a mess. That's usually how my dreams are, and I hate it. I would like to have cool dreams where I am the queen of Sheba or something, but that doesn't happen. If we have karma in the dream state, that is a totally new piece of information that I haven't heard anywhere else. But I know it's true if they say it.

It's hard to imagine, but lots of things are hard to imagine. We have to be discerning about what we came here to do. The dream states will tell us more of that. But I don't think we need to run around telling people the stuff that we can't prove. Can I prove that I see all these beings and that I have gargoyles in here? No, I can't. I sound psychotic. Maybe I am. But I'm going to make light of it. And I will never tell people they have to do something or it's absolute truth. All I say is this is my experience.

What I want to do is to help other people to understand their experiences, not try to act like a damn guru. People are trying to set boundaries with this stuff that you can't see and that you can't touch. How do you set a boundary with that? Well, there are rules that God sets for all the all the icky stuff. Even the demonic have to play by God's rules. They have to go by the rules.

They can't just interfere, but what makes us delicious to these bad experiences is that we have magnetic imprints in us. An example of these magnetic imprints is I used to be the kind of person who, if I was in a grocery line, would attract every needy, codependent, whiny person in the store. The kind of people that are going to tell me everything because I'm like delicious to that. So, I put up a boundary around that, and that doesn't happen anymore.

We are all growing and progressing. That's a practical thing. I can see that, and I can prove it by my life and my behavior. But this other woo-woo stuff, you can't see it or prove it. And that is what hooks people in. That's why people get involved in cults or with unsavory gurus. There are some wonderful ones out there. So, let's just try to be honest. Let's try to be as impeccable and as honest as we can be.

It can be hard enough for any of us to be totally honest all the time. It's our authenticity. We have to keep clearing the past and the programming that doesn't work. Some programming does work. Some of it that we need. But not all of it works, and people are different. It might be okay for one person or not for the other person. But there are certain things in society that work, such as laws, that are important. Are they all good? No, but it's pretty important to follow as many as we can because they're there for a reason.

It keeps us from falling into violence. When people have been enslaved or starved, instead of the abused becoming the abuser, they are going to have to forgive, which means moving on. It doesn't mean what happened is okay. It means moving on for yourself. And that is why we're seeing all this violence. We can't seem to move on. We're dumb. We cannot do it. We just have to go through the same thing over and over and over again.

We're going from one extreme to the other. And that's what we are trying not to do as spiritual people. But when we lie and try to present ourselves as high and mighty or gurus, that is deception, and that's one extreme. And eventually, that'll fall off.

The truth always comes out. So, I found out at age ten. When I was a kid, I was a big fat liar. I was hysterically funny because I just made up my own world. Nobody could believe anything I said. But I saw these weird things, and I would say I saw them, and they were true, but nobody could see them. Because of that, then I just started lying. I was a kid. Are we supposed to grow out of that? I hope I did.

We're all a work in progress. And it drives me crazy. Can I figure anything out and have it stick? Things are changing so fast right now. But great truths are coming out. Look at the people protesting all over the planet. People power is coming up, and that is what will change things. Our ability to speak out and to act and to do things that we think will change the planet, to change our community, to change our life, our family; that's what's important.

It doesn't have to be big. We just have to try. Millions of people all over the planet are starting to speak out, and we're seeing these monopolies at the top fall apart. That's been prophesied for centuries. And that's why it's chaotic. There's nothing out there that's solid to grab onto right now.

We haven't made it yet. That's why Ray 1, the Ray of destruction, is so necessary. And while that is active, it works with the other rays. Ray 4 is artistic. It's a bunch of colors. Ray 6 is very political. But that Ray 1 just destroys the old so that we can rebuild.

I'm very hopeful. And *Share International* also expresses this optimism. Maitreya says, "I know you will hear me when I come out." He has seen it. The thing that grieves him the most is the complacency of the starving millions. And that's what his number one priority is: feeding people. Food and potable water. And it'll happen quickly.

I have hope, and everything that I harp on in all these personal subjects is just me trying to figure out my piece in it. And by God, everybody has to figure out their own piece of it. Everybody's piece is a little different.

If you want to be different, just be yourself because there's nobody like you. We can all be special little snowflakes and get in line, but that does nothing. That's the old way. And that's what's dying out. It's scary to be yourself authentically.

zoliartexoticamontana.com/music

Child of the Sun

Understanding the Urgency of Dreams

We don't always remember our dreams or access what we learned from them because we're in a different world. We really are in the emotional world when we dream. It feels to me that dreamscapes shift too quickly to allow time to consciously sit with them in the dream proper. How often in a dream do we recall sitting down on a couch with a cup of tea and recall taking time to process the previous weird ass event?

I believe that the subconscious knows everything about us and recalls each experience precisely. But our physical senses cross boundaries with each other, trying to cognate the event. The environmental scent may be overwhelmed by a visual or the visual by a noise. That's the astral world. In dreams, we seem to depend on skills from the dream world senses.

In the dream state, we don't have access to the five physical senses that we have here. And they play off each other here, such as if I smell a skunk, I know it's a skunk. It's either that or some bad marijuana. The brain connects that, and then we visually look for it, and maybe we're listening to where the skunk is, or the pothead, or whatever.

Certainly, there are times when we have all the senses alive and aware, but it usually seems to be visual and auditory. I'm not sure about that, but when we just wake up and feel that sense of urgency, it's a sign that there is something very important to pay attention to. And it's important to note that when you do pay attention to the dreams, you remember more of them.

Energy created is not destroyed. So, we are creating a pathway for these dreams to come through in our minds. It's like a question mark. And whenever we're curious about something that's magnetic, we will attract the electric composite of that. I think the electricity, in this sense, is the dream. I hope.

It connects just like electricity.

> ***Energy created is not destroyed. So, we are creating a pathway for these dreams to come through in our minds.***

Writing dreams down does make a big difference. I don't do that because, as a psychic medium, I go into that other state and kind of stay in that, and it's hard for me to find the words, but your subconscious knows everything. And what we're trying to do is to bring it into the conscious realm. The more that we practice it when they teach these dream courses, like at the Monroe Institute to other patients, they say to pay attention to it, write it down, and ask for things to happen in your dream.

In other words, ask to see a three-foot pink boulder. And when you see that three-foot pink boulder, you will realize you are dreaming. Now, I've tried that. I'm no good at it. I'm just not, but there are people that really can do that sort of thing. And I guess it takes practice.

In no way do I think I'm an expert on any of this. It's just my opinion and my experience hopefully to either irritate people enough or to make them curious enough to want to figure it out themselves.

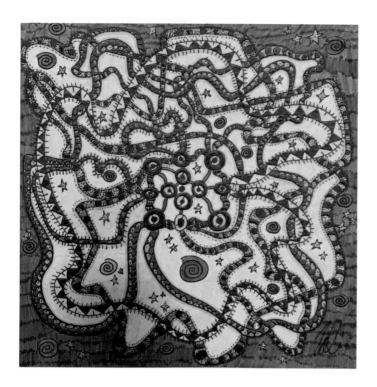

Your Questions Answered:
Why does it feel like the world is going crazy?

Globally, we are in such a weirdly transformative era. I've spoken to numerous people that have asked, what is going on? People are cranky. I'm having an awful time.

Everything feels a bit off because the old dying forms compete and claw at time to let them stay past their death date. There is so much new coming in that we are just overloaded.

It seems like everything's going crazy all at once. Crazy is chaos, and it brings change. The chaos is the change. It's Pluto. It's Uranus. It's the Aquarian age. We just have to get used to it.

There is horrible stuff happening all the time. But we have to look at this and go on what the Masters say. The Masters of Wisdom are not all ascended, but they are Masters. They finished Earth school, and they're still here to help us because we're so messed up. They're saying everything's fine, everything's going well. We're waiting for Maitreya to be able to come out into the open for the day of declaration. That is what's going to change everything.

It is like a birth fury. That's what I think we're going through. We are going through the birth canal, and we can't see what's ahead. It absolutely explains a lot of people's frantic and almost irrational behavior.

It's fear. Everything is either love or fear. And if people haven't done their work, if they're drinking, drugging, doing all this stuff, they can't get control of themselves or their emotional body is running things that's a problem. I used to think I was going to figure everything out. I don't think that anymore. That's part of my stress right now. I keep doing all this inner work, this health work, and like everyone else I want what I want immediately. We get to these points of closure with the past, and we have to wait for the new to come in.

And while we're waiting, it can be very uncomfortable. And I think that's where we are globally. And we're not very patient in our waiting, so we make it more uncomfortable for ourselves. We all want what we want right now. We want the endorphins. We want serotonin. We want to feel good.

I'm going through a learning curve of just settling into detachment, and for God's sake, Zoli, chill! How about you? I hope you're doing better with this than yours truly. I believe in you, remember. You can't really fix things. You can't change that much, but you can put yourself out there as a sacrifice to your ego.

That's a tough one when your nature is to want to fix things or to change things. How much of this really is just human nature? It's what you get to go through in Earth school, and you're not going to change it. We're not going to change the seasons. That's what I always come back to. If you learn to flow with the seasons instead of complaining about the weather every day, then what's going on out there is less important than what's going on in here.

There's a great wisdom in deception because deception, if we realize it, will lead us to truth. Most times we really can't recognize the truth unless we've been deceived or we think about the deception. And I think that's very much what's happening right now in this world. The unrest with these great structures that are changing.

Maitreya said thirty years ago, your beloved structures of the world are going to go away. The things that we trusted, government, religion, these big belief systems, education, everything's up for change. And what is the change? The change is human beings taking control of themselves and their lives.

We all have desire getting in the way. Desire is our challenge. That's the emotional body, that's the astral realm, and it had run us ever since Atlantis. Ever since we did such a good job of integrating emotion into the physicality, it's still running us. We're trying to be mental. We're trying to get to the mental realm. It's more scientific, more clear-headed.

Why do you think there are different sides stoking the dismissive polarities of opposites? It seems like it's stopping us from learning and evolving. Personal reasons are part of why we resist change. But globally, there are some pretty nasty icky forces out there that don't want you to wake up. They want to be sure that you can be controlled, where there is going to be from putting chemicals in your body specifically, putting ideas in your body, belief systems, and these are very, very powerful negative forces. And right now, they know they're losing.

Do you want to have hope? They're losing. They say the devil is in the details. Well, the details are losing, and we're coming to a time where there are going to be more people awake than not. And I don't mean a level of genius awake, but more of the idea that wait a minute, I can do something about this.

The old system is dead. The old age started dying out in 1625 with the new age coming in 1675. So, it's dead. It's done. We are in the Aquarian age. And Aquarian doesn't like to be controlled.

I personally think that's the ticket. I mean, it's change, you guys. Real palatable change, gut-wrenching, home-wrecking change. How much are we going to resist the change? What do I have to give up? What is comfortable? What can't I give up? What economically can I do?

We're starting to feel more, to face offering our authenticity to the mass public arena. That vulnerability is chewing at the edges of this change. This is the 1960's on steroids. Radically transformative, unfamiliar, truth-revealing and raw. But hold on there, we have to remember these times have been prophesied for millennia. They're SUPPOSED to occur. Our emotions are the enemy, ouch.

It's going to be kind of crazy on steroids, but it's all for the good, and you're going to see amazing things happen. I think Elon Musk's company is getting ready to present brain implants for people who are paralyzed to make them be able to walk again. You don't hear about all the good stuff. That'll be the start of the medical changes so people can actually get health care.

Right now, everything's about the almighty dollar, and that is what's going to change. I don't know how it's going to change. I'm not a seer. I don't know how it's going to shift. But it's shifting gradually. I don't know if it's a Bitcoin. I'm not sure how it's going to happen, but it will happen. Will the stock markets go down? I don't know.

Something has to shift all over to the world, but it's going to take Maitreya coming out to the open. It will have to be something that immense.

Though we are reaching the cusp, we're seeing it happen now. Still, it's gradual. The more people can communicate with each other all over the world, on the internet, on Twitter, on TikTok, and all these sites. The more people can communicate the more truth will come out. That's the beauty of that, and that's not going away. It will increase as more and more of us awaken to express our true selves. Our communication with others will become more authentic because WE have become more authentic. You'll see huge changes in economics and politics, social values and structures.

There will still be plenty of people that are just going to be jerks. It's just human nature. But I guarantee, oh yes, things are changing for the better. We just don't see it. But it's slow. It's really weird because it's happening very fast, but it's all so slow. Let me explain what I mean by that. These changes that push us are intense and we're living with the fire of this intensity. But it's a slow intensity.

It has to catch up. Human nature has to catch up to the changes, see. That's what feels slow about it. It does have that odd quality of feeling both fast and slow at the same time.

Life is everything, honey. It's never just one thing. It's good. It's bad. It's ugly. It's exquisite. It's everything. But one thing that has to change in this world is the lack of equity and opportunity for people. Our Constitution says all men are born equal. You're born equal, and you have the opportunity to pursue happiness. You don't get it. You have an opportunity to pursue that.

And what we're trying to get to is a world where there is no one starving. People have a place to live. Then you have education, then you have social structures, and then you have arts. We're going to get there. And it's just not pretty how we're getting there.

We're doing things the hard way. That's what we do. We're dumb. We just can't stop. I've been very frustrated with that lately, maybe with myself, I don't know, but very frustrated with the world that we just keep making these same mistakes over and over again. We just can't seem to get it right.

It seems like the same things are happening over and over and over again, even though we know the outcome. We will see change. The people will demand the change, and it will happen. It will come because they're starting to realize their representatives are not doing their jobs.

How is it that you're a normal person, then you get you get into politics and you become a millionaire? How'd you do that? I thought you were a public servant. It's all about the money. So, it's a really sad state of affairs. Everything is the almighty dollar.

That's why I charge a little below what other people are charging out there. It removes the barrier to accessing the work. Maybe if you need it, it's going to help you.

Your Questions Answered:
Why do nightmares feel so intense?

Fear. That's it. In nightmares, your fear is palatable, but you can't always define the reason. Sometimes, we're just afraid of the wrong things. With all of the nasty evil crap out there fully deserving of our fear, we often focus on the most ridiculous perceptions as a threat.

When I catch myself reacting rather than responding, I feel silly and attempt to backpedal into calmer waters. The water of emotion, that is. But why do irrational fears pop up in our dreams? That's a different landscape altogether.

Superstitions, religious or political dogmas, can grab onto our fear handle and yank us off the calm ride we were on a second ago. What IS that? The emotional body blows up like a balloon on its way to exploding, exposing us to the next level of fear which is flight. We freeze and try to run away before needing to fight our way out of it. That's the stuff of nightmares.

So, what's going on? Fear is the raw edge of emotional control. How do we escape it? If awake, we can try to logic it and calm our way down the ladder of escalated drama. But in nightmares, where is that mental piece? The icky energies weaken the mind with emotional weapons, dislodging us from comfort with no exit except to awaken from the astral discomfort.

It is spiritual gaslighting presented by none other than the unconscious speck of dirt under the bed harboring monsters. We seem to have an agreement with horror to awaken the logic and disillusionment with shock and awe. We crave the solace and control of mentally addressing the screen with the balm of logic that is the frontal brain piece of discernment lacking in the limbic system's toolbox.

Why do we scare ourselves silly when we contain the weapons of disillusionment in the same body? We scare ourselves more than anyone else could because of this specific agreement we have with the physical body to protect it. Does the physical have its own consciousness? Some say it does.

Uncertainty can breed fear. Its offspring live in our nightmares. And nightmares are the stuff of uncertainty. Why do we transport all that stuff of nightmarish drama back into our waking self? Many say these nightmares are messages from our unconscious.

No one is pulling the strings but us, at least that part of us hiding somewhere within. The fears habituating the lower two astral planes bleed into our breakfast cereal, reminding us of unfinished business with the self.

Most of the nightmares I recall experiencing lacked any sensory revelations other than the visual or auditory. I don't recall smelling or tasting anything. How about you? All senses acutely stressed in the astral can be accessed in a similar way to our waking state.

If Billy Bob is grilling pork steaks next door, maybe a memory of that smell would be recalled in a dream. That stuff seems to be common. But if our five physical senses are rightly lodged in the physical world, how does that cross-over occur? Ideas?

No matter how you look at it, you are slap in the middle of your emotional body during nightmares. And they happen for a reason. They are pointing a finger at a specific issue that we're not getting or that we're afraid of.

My big thing is abandonment. I have had those nightmares of being in the city and abandoned. I can't find anybody. Where does abandonment come from? I was never abandoned. I was adopted, but I went right from my birth mother to mom and dad. A lot of times, we will have these things from past lives that come up over and over again, certain themes, so to speak.

When we have nightmares, they're often on the same theme. Sometimes, we'll have the dream of being naked in the city without any clothes. Well, that's clearly vulnerability. Or being chased by something. What in our life is chasing us?

There is a kind of logic to it, but the nightmare feels so intense because you are in your emotional body, and there's nothing to stop it. Your mental body is not active when you're in the astral realm. It's all emotion. And when you're in the physical body here, and your consciousness is here, for good or ill, you can access your mind and tell yourself to cut it out. You need to be able to see that there's nothing chasing you. If you look behind you, they're going the other direction. In nightmares, we don't seem to logic it out in the dream. It's just all emotion.

zoliartexoticamontana.com/music

Baby, Who's Your Fantasy?

C'hin Lao: Messages from the Astral Realm

What would you do if you clearly saw a wizened Chinese man sitting on your couch one morning? I freaked. This was at the farm in 1998. The farm portals were like the Star Wars cantina in the movie. Beings from other places came in and out of these portals to rest.

I saw them a lot. They often told me stories or presented ideas that I was advised to research, to write down and keep them in a safe place. That went on for the twenty-five years I lived there. So, this Chinese dude said his name was C'hin Lao. He was very calm, very sweet, and quite detached. He, along with a bunch of other discarnates and higher 3D level folks, gave me most of the material I published in the Reality Pirate Newsletter.

Am I sure who they were? No, I'm not. But what I can promise you, though, is that the writings were dictated from them to me by my furiously scribbling hand. The energy signature of channeled reception is quite different from those of the fourth chakra or above. I can't really explain it except it's very emotional. The differences are acute. I'm not a fan of anyone following channeled stuff because we can't be sure who it is. In fact, don't follow anything unless you feel it totally from your heart.

The astral entities can themselves believe that they are angels, and they can tell you that. But they lie. They don't know they lie, but they lie.

The astral entities can they themselves believe that they are angels, and they can tell you that, but they lie. They don't know they lie, but they lie. So, please read these channels' texts as stories and attitudes from someone or something very loving but not from Zoli's brain. I continue to wonder, if any, if these beings are who they say they are or were. Could they be projections from my own various lifetimes? Possibly. Are they holograms from some way out-there place? From me in the future or the past? Or maybe from you? I don't know.

But they are loving and kind and tickle reality with vibrancy and joy.

Your Questions Answered: What are recurring dreams?

Recurring dreams happen because you didn't get it yet. There's a message in it. It depends on the kind of dream, though.

For probably thirty years, I had a recurring dream. A recurring dream can be stress, or it can be messages from the other side. It can also be us going to the same place on the astral realm with other people. But my dream has improved over the years. When I have that recurring dream now, I am in control of me there.

It started out when I was in my early twenties, and I would be in a strange city with no purse. I didn't speak the language. Nobody would help me. I had no suitcase, nothing. I could not get out. I couldn't get home. And this went on for years and years and years. In my twenties is when I started doing a lot of therapy and help work. By resolving that sort of fear in myself over the years, it got better to where I would be sitting in the back of a car and realizing I was in a strange city, and I would be able to ask for help. Or I would be in a city, and I realized it wasn't strange.

So, now, when I have that recurring dream, I'm in control. I find myself driving the car, or I will be standing, and I'm very verbal and I'm able to ask for help. Those kinds of recurring dreams are real messages from what I call recovery self when we are picking up lost pieces. We're learning more about ourselves, and we're picking up pieces about our soul. It's sometimes to gain awareness or acceptance about yourself.

It's a really varied situation. The recurring dreams that are terrifying, that are like nightmares, those are our fears. They can be from this life or another, trying to get us to reason with the fear part of our self because, remember, the astral realm is all emotion.

Fear is all below the heart. It's usually in the gut. So, a lot more things can happen in the astral realm that could be dangerous, and you probably won't die from it as you would here. Running down a dark alley with zombies chasing you with five-inch knives. In the dream, you'll wake up.

Another kind of recurring dream is where we are giving ourselves messages about what we want to do during the next day. In our so-called dream state, we do some of that. We look at options of what's available to us the next day. That's a lot of what déjà vu really is.

Your Questions Answered: Why is logic so skewed in our dreams?

It is imperative to differentiate between the logic available in our so-called waking state and that of the dream state. The dream world is much more transitory. In the waking world, we have our five physical senses to add color to events. These senses define experience in mind, body and spirit. But in the dream state we seem to move quickly from one scene to the next, devoid often of the input of all five senses. The logic of the dream world is transitory and apparently uncontrollable.

Logic deglamorizes emotion. Logic says, "Wait a minute. You think that chair just turned into a cow? That's a dream thing." It can happen, but in the physical world, it's not going to happen. It's kind of a cultic belief system that you can do anything you want; you can change anything you want. Well, no, you can't.

The logic in dreams is not there. We don't have that piece, and I find that very intriguing. In the physical world, we depend on these physical senses. And we depend on the brain/mind to cognate and make sense out of the world. We want to know what is happening. And in the dream world, things happen so fast. We can't seem to get a grip on what is going on. Experiences are acute and chronic. But here, we have time to say I'm going to close the door and sit on the toilet for two hours and just be by myself.

You can't do that in the dream world. I don't know of anybody that does that because of the quick action of the dream world. There's no time wasted because there's not really time in that sense.

At least, that's what I think happens. But we lack something in that other world that we depend on so heartily for here. And it's a beautiful agreement that we have that we're going to depend on these physical senses.

We recognize things by their edges. And in the dream world, those things can morph. They can change just like an LSD trip, which I don't want.

Time almost doesn't exist in dreams. It only exists in the way that we relate to what happened. In the physical world, we agree to time. It's Saturn, Capricorn. Saturn rules time, and Father time is what Capricorn has been called. It rules restriction and regulation. And you don't have that in the other world. The dream world is ruled by Neptune. That's Pisces. That is woo-woo land. It is out there. And it doesn't have any boundaries except for the ones that we create. And we refer to those limits when we're trying to make sense of it.

We use our human waking logic to try to make sense of the dreams, and that's part of why they're so hard to discern. The sense of urgency escalates when we wake up, and we have that information to relate it to the physical world. We have to relate it to time and space, and all of a sudden, we're trying to corral it and falsely box it in from a time that had no boxes.

Psychologists frequently recommend that we not worry too much about the content of the dream, but focus on what we felt. What did the dream evoke? The dream of me on the bike with that girlfriend, with that guy telling me I had no power to achieve my goals. I refused to let him stop me. I didn't believe what I was being told, and I was just going to be courageous and go on. That was the feeling that I had for that dream.

As a short aside: Lucifer is from Saturn, and he came to this planet over a million years ago. There were also great beings from all of the planets in our solar system, from Mars, Venus, Jupiter, Uranus, and Neptune. Pluto is not yet at that point of anyone wanting them here. But there were all these beings that came here to help develop humanity.

During the time of Atlantis, Lucifer himself was the most suited for this world because of time and space. Saturn rules that, and Lucifer/ Satan was a master at it. Lucifer means light bearer. He was scheduled to teach humanity all the skills, all the psychic sciences, all the arts, all the music, writing, and math. He was scheduled to teach that because he was most adept at dealing with this Earth. He was energetically connected. But every time he incarnated, over a period of hundreds of thousands of years in Atlantis, he became more and more addicted to the physical. Mastering time and space, he became evil. He controlled people, including most of the people on Atlantis. The reason it blew up was because most of the people of Atlantis followed him.

They let go of spirituality. They let go of anything that wasn't control. There were hybrids created between animals, humans, and plant life, pitiful creatures like the centaur and the mermaid. There was evil done with animals and plants and people that don't belongs in this book. Finally, a great war happened between the forces of materiality called evil, who believed Lucifer and those who were against Lucifer, called Hierarchy, the light forces. There were so very few of the light bearers left then. Atlantis exploded and sank under the ocean. But reality was at a standstill, a tie of sorts undecided at best.

Lucifer stayed on Earth, and he still impacted humanity, including World War I and World War II. That was what we call Armageddon. And that is different from what will happen in two thousand years when humanity will forever get rid of evil on this planet.

But that was Lucifer who did that. And there were millions of people who were his followers from Atlantis who helped him. And Hitler himself created a religion where he took over Jesus' place. He got rid of the Old Testament. And Lucifer is doing all this to say he was god. So, Hitler, who was the number one channel for Lucifer, got rid of Christianity, and there were churches with Hitler's picture as the new Jesus, and he was white with blue eyes. There is every evil that you can imagine.

When World War II was about to end, the Axis powers were given the formula for the bomb by the Masters. And that ended that. On October 17th, 1947, Lucifer, who is now Satan, was sent back to Saturn. He's not even here. The so-called devil hasn't been here since 1947. Then, how about the time and space that he was trying to control? How do you then explain all the crap in the world? It's people.

All his little minions, the demons, the evil shit that people do, the purgatorial souls are still doing his work. Just because he isn't here, that doesn't mean it's not happening. The good part of this is he's now sent back to Saturn, where he has to start over. Saturn is the hardest planet to live on. Why is that? It's all about time and space. It's restriction. The dream world doesn't have that restriction.

In the future, Lucifer will bring all of those people that he corrupted back up through the line of evolution to Saturn. Saturn is the hardest place to go. It is ruled by time and space. The fact that both of those are so prominent on this Earth explains why it's so easy to get into any addiction. Addiction lets us believe we are in control and that we can rule time and space.

Anytime I hear a priest who is exorcising demons and whatever it is comes out and says that they're Satan, and I know those demonic forces are not. They're liars. Satan is not even here, but who knows that? It's great theater to have him still here.

That's why there's so much light that is able to come into this planet now, and we'll be fine. We'll get through this. Maitreya will come out, he will guide us, he will teach us, we'll be fine. Right now, it's pretty damn bad, but usually it's the darkest before the dawn.

zoliartexoticamontana.com/music

The Beauty Way

The Dream World

What comes to mind when you hear the word dream? It kind of takes you out of your daily mindset, doesn't it? The dream world includes daydreams as well as those events during sleep when we sort of shoot out of the physical body, attached to the silver cord from our abdomen. But what are daydreams, and why are they called dreams? We shift our consciousness to a density different from the one we use to keep from being kicked by the moose charging from the bog. We need to be here and attend to the so-called real world to be able to remain in it, right?

When someone says, "Hey! Earth to Zoli..." Where does our mind go? When we disconnect and break from the space-time normalcy, that is what I define as daydreaming. Our mind visits somewhere else, where I don't know, but it can be other densities, other dimensions, other worlds, other anywhere but here, at least what we call here when running from the moose. We seem to connect dreams with a kind of freedom. We like freedom because there is so little of it. When we dream or daydream, we just aren't here. Freedom from here can be an endorphin delight.

Except for the icky dreams, our reveries present an alternative to all that stuff we have to do: our responsibilities, our pains, and our dramas. But oh, in those dreams, we can be anywhere in our minds and imagine a better world. Someone once told me that imagination is "image in action." Sounds true. When a kid is happy and jumps up and down and escapes the gravitational field, even for a few seconds is pure joy. Gravity is, well, grave.

Our feet must walk on the ground, not be lighter than air. It's the agreement we have with this reality. Gravity is the great equalizer. But when we dream, sometimes we might fly. Other times, we see ourselves from other perspectives. Dreams are limitless, while we are limited in the physical world. We come here to learn, to limit ourselves with the constraints of life, seeking to recall the freedom of life before life. I know a few folks who claim that we can do anything we want at any time if only we've imagined it hard enough. That is an abstract ideal, a sweet thought and a Neptunian fantasy in search of freedom.

The agreements of physical life may escape us once we evolve past the fourth initiation. There are only a couple hundred of those guys incarnate these days. But in our dreams, we can idealize and abstract all we want. No harm there. That third chakra astral connection is a Petri dish for our creative self. Both afferent and efferent energies pour through that center of emotion.

That third chakra petri dish is ripe with the feeling nature we seek, and sensitive types fall into the trap of the desire body. That desire body, the astral, is the sensation-seeking pleasure center.

Drugs and alcohol alter perception and discernment of reception. Artists are creative folks who seek inspiration and often believe inspiration comes from losing frontal brain discernment. I don't happen to agree with that belief, but we are allowed to be inventive and creative and spontaneous in art, so why not experience that? It's a phase we endure when young or when we are searching for our true selves.

All highs lose altitude sooner or later. They can be prolonged with substance, but the price is higher than the high. I prefer to maintain a clear head and an undrugged frontal lobe, but maybe I'm wrong. The astral emotional world is that dream, that high, that vacation from the norm. What price do we pay for illusion and delusion? Maitreya says that the greatest drug is detachment. When I do that, my life goes great.

What about the mediumship madness of the mid to late 1800s? Why was channeling and chatting with dead people so fashionable? The Masters of Wisdom tried an experiment. They do that a lot. They opined that if folks could experience the astral realm through materializations, perhaps it would serve to turn the tables from the gross materialism and industrialization replacing belief in Spirit and truth? It didn't work, by the way. The spiritualist movement did nothing but create the fanaticism around material phenomena and ghost calling. Life is truly a conglomerate of experiments.

> *But when we dream, sometimes we might fly. Other times, we see ourselves from other perspectives. Dreams are limitless, while we are limited in the physical world.*

Some of the Masters thought that the purely materialistic and avarice-based consciousness in the Western world was not yet ready or receptive to the ancient wisdom teachings or the texts that are written a million years ago in the lost language of Sensar. But perhaps they could choose a high initiate, a disciple to at least try.

There's that try thing again. Each century or so, the Masters choose one of their disciples to disseminate intellectual arcane knowledge to press forward our mundane consciousness. That time, they chose the irascible Helena Petrovna Blavatsky. As a 4th Degree Initiate who had been tried and tested for many lifetimes, was now capable of mediating, not channeling, but mediating and receiving the words pressed to her by her Master. I label reception of higher power from the heart center and above as MEDIATION. Remember, channeling is a third chakra emotional event. Helena did not do that, period.

Master Kuthumi was also a purveyor of these teachings. He believed humanity was ready to believe what we could incorporate at least some of the ancient teachings, hopefully enough to abate the rise of evil presented soon as a great world war. World War I and World War II were actually one war. The Materially evil energies, Satanic power, went underground after World War II. That is a good reason to have options about what we can create in the real world.

We do so by resonating with similar energies. It can be karmic, Uranus, or Neptune. No one really won that Great War because the Icky Ones retreated to regroup and choose their own disciple, who was the evil personality called Adolf Hitler. After WWII, the awful negativity entered the stock markets and negative aspects of world governments, where they remain to this day.

One more thing about Hitler you need to know. The German people are very mediumistic and gifted in the psychic arts. Hitler was a high medium who was capable of being overshadowed by the forces of evil during his maniac speeches. Power used by evil is force. If Hierarchy had not given the formula for the bomb to the Allied powers, we would have Nazi flags flying all over the world today.

Enough said. Icky stuff. So, the mid to late 1800s swam in the astral pond with mediums apporting objects, some real, but mostly fake and theatrical shows. Channels dove into the psychic pond while the Masters watched, disappointed that we, the people, still focused on the physical phenomena in lieu of the magic heart, creating what we needed to do from within, not without. We still to this day rebuke the so-called invisible supernatural truths unless we can prove it with our only three levels of testing solid, liquid and physical gaseous substances.

Blavatsky mediated the book *ISIS Unveiled* and *The Secret Doctrine*. These brilliant messenger books opened doorways to previously undiscernible paths to real truth. So, that worked, kind of. Only those with eyes to see and hearts to feel could follow the inner road and choose discernment over delusion. Do you think these great ancient teachings should show up in dreams? Sure, they do. These are the same archetypes and cornerstones for all of humanity from 18.5 million years ago until forever.

We can and do access tidbits, but only if we have the receptors developed enough to receive and recognize the signs and symbols. I believe that no one can teach anyone. We only learn what we are ready to receive. What symbols appear in your dreams? You may be getting more than you know.

Your Questions Answered:
Can agreements be broken?

We do it all the time. It's called karma. Everything has repercussions. It depends on what kind of agreement you're talking about: the little ones or the big ones. It depends on who it is and what it is.

There are big ones and little ones. It's one thing if I'm going to meet you at the movie theater at two and you never show up. Nothing is equal in that way. But if you have an agreement to come to Earth to do a certain thing and you don't do it, well, you'll come back and do it some other time. But what or who did you disappoint by not doing it?

It is multilevel. That's a very complex situation because every situation is different. The lords of karma control everything in that way.

I certainly am not the one to pontificate on it because it's extremely complex.

There are consequences for absolutely everything we do, and it has to come from our intention and the effect of what we did. Sometimes there are certain things that were pushed towards the line. Even if we try to pull away from them, perhaps these are ties that can't be broken.

Some things are irresistible. Somebody meets another person, and a month later, they're married. How does that happen? These are irresistible things and then we blame ourselves for being married to a jerk, or they were married to us who was the jerk. Everything is karmic, and we come back over and over again to try to get out of all the dogma that we get attached to. But the agreements can be very subtle.

My prayer every day is, "I give you my word that I'll do what I came here to do and more." What scares me more than anything in the world is me not keeping my agreements, probably because in lifetimes in the past, I didn't.

It's more complex than we seem to understand. It's that old conundrum that everything's planned from the beginning, and then we have free will. Both are true. And if everything's happening at once simultaneously, like in the movie *Outlander*, where you can be in the past and the future, you're all living one life in different times. We don't have the ability to really get that. We can explain it intellectually like a matrix situation, but we don't get it.

We have to be almost at the level of a Master to get that, and we're not. So, we have to be patient with our slow selves. That's always the answer like the Ho'oponopono prayer. "I love you, I'm sorry. Please forgive me. Thank you." I had to say it to myself the other day because I was just beating the crap out of myself about not being able to do absolutely everything perfectly as if I knew how.

Forgiving yourself is probably the hardest thing. It all starts with that. Forgiving any other person really is forgiving ourselves. Though, people run into a conundrum with it. There are different interpretations of what forgiveness is. Do you say "I forgive you," meaning what you did is okay? Or "I forgive you," meaning, it's not okay what you did, but I'm just not going to think about it anymore? Or "I forgive you," and I don't know if it's okay or not. I haven't resolved it, but I'm just not going to be around you. There are different interpretations of that.

You can weaponize it. I had a situation a while back where this man was just really aggressive with me. And I basically told him if he did it again, he would take a walk with Emma and me (Emma is my S and W M4) to further address his assholeness. Never did it, but boundaries are sacrosanct. Many times, we say we are sorry but are really sorry for getting caught. He said, "I'm sorry. Can you forgive me?"

And I said, "No. Why should I forgive you that? You knew exactly what you were saying. You know why you said what you did. You hurt my feelings, and you were obnoxious, and you didn't care until I caught you and called you on it."

He said, "Well, you know, it's the Christian thing to do."

I said, "That's not my brand of Christianity."

That didn't go well. And I still think he's a jerk, but he probably thinks I'm a jerk too. So what? He didn't come within ten feet of me anymore. That's for sure. I joke about it and say, "Here in Montana, we're all armed. So, not much goes on here in Montana."

That's why there are many different places in the world to live. And why do we live in certain places? It's usually karmic. We're there to do certain work or to be with certain people.

Your Questions Answered: Are aliens living our reality?

Well, let's back it up a little bit. What is an alien? I call them off-worlders. Those are people from our solar system—Venus, Jupiter, Uranus, Saturn, Mars, but not Pluto. They aren't allowed here because they are barbaric, the worst of humanity on Earth. There are humanoid people living on all planets of our solar system, but they may not look exactly alike. And so, they can come and be in our reality, but not in their physical bodies. This isn't exactly correct, but it's like they live in the astral world, and we live in the physical world.

Because they exist in a non-Earth, physical structural environment. We are in a thick density here. The physical world is so in our face that we depend too heavily upon the five outer senses. And it's a good thing we have them. But those living in finer, lighter places are less emotionally and mentally heavy than Earth folks.

There is also the difference in actual etheric atmosphere. I mean, what the heck do they breathe? It's probably not a carbon-oxygen-based air. What do you think? These things differ us from them. The gravitational fields are different. There are all sorts of variations specific to each planetary system. It is quite complex, more than my little brain can grok.

So, the physical Earth animal bodies we live in are dense. But Pluto is a nasty place of un-evolved anger and fear. What the heck do they look like? What is that place about? It sounds like an imagined version of a hell, but who really knows? You cannot see these other beings that are from other places.

Are there other Earths? There are ten and a half billion suns in the Milky Way. Everything is out there. But this place is guarded and this solar system that we have is very precious. Earth is the only planet here that has created a Christ. That's very big. That is huge. And so, we are being watched. We're not going to be allowed to blow the planet up. That's going to affect everything.

They are here all of the time. Are they walking among us? There are a few who are born into Earth bodies because their mission is to assimilate and be here for years. They'd have little difficulty with physical assimilation because they are in an Earth form, see? Some of those Off-worlders are actual Avatars, a highly-evolved being from one of the higher planets in our solar system. Examples are Leonardo Da Vinci, Moses, Sai Baba, Maria Callas, as well as several composers and scientists. They dropped to Earth under the karmic law of service, sacrificing by agreeing to enlighten and improve humanity by suffering in a place of lower evolution than they come from. Do Avatars go to other planets? What do you think?

Some Off-worlders agree to assignments on Earth for hours, days, weeks or months. Depending on their origin, their bodily structure and degree of atmospheric protection, they can remain here temporarily to get 'er done. It must be like going to a foreign country with minimal intel, uncomfortable accommodations and a raw energy of unfamiliarity. We are indebted to these gentle beings who sacrifice so readily to assist us. Someday, these debts will have to be paid.

They ARE here, but it's pretty rare. In the interior of our planet are ancient bases from which their ships come and go. They are absolutely harmless. They clean up the massive amounts of radiation, pollution and other by-products of our stupidity. Their only mission is service to us, even to the ridiculously terrified emotional idiots who fear them. Indeed, they have been here for millennia but increasingly since our messing around with nuclear power around the 1940's. Our ability to destroy the planet affects the entire solar system. But walking on Earth, why would they want to do that? What is the point?

They communicate with us by telepathy. You get ideas in your mind, and they can understand your ideas telepathically. It's a skill of high intuition which is externally located in the Ajna center or sixth chakra. All chakras are in the etheric sheath surrounding your physical body, an exact replica of your physical one but electromagnetic in nature.

During the 20 years I telepathically worked with the Zeta Reticuli and Fish Man (refer to my first book, *The Reality Pirate's Journal*), I saw pictures in my mind which were intel from these off-worlders teaching me what they identified as IDP, Interdimensional Physics. Most of their commo was fast-paced, non-emotional and crisply clear. They weren't physically there, but when they were etheretically around, it was like I could taste metal. It was a very crisp, acidic type feeling and taste. And it's hard to explain. But there is a presence.

People think humans are going to Mars. Well, that's ridiculous. The planet itself is useless because the people on it are not physical. They're etheric. They're there; we just can't see them.

Why would you want to send people to Mars? What is the point of doing that? There are four finer frequencies, energetic locals, above our Earthly understanding of solids, liquids and physical gas. That's where all this other energy is, and that's where the other beings are when they come here. We're so stuck in what we can see, smell, hear, taste, and feel.

That's just the physical body, but we're not our physical body. We have our consciousness in it. But we are a lot more than that. At The Monroe Institute, participants first enroll in the Gateway Program, where they receive a document that begins with, "I am more than my physical body." It goes on to talk about how you have the ability to go into the densities and other dimensions and remain aware of experience. We do it a lot, and we're not aware of it. That's the daydream thing.

zoliartexoticamontana.com/music

Jesus, Sing to Me

Meeting Twelve Archetypes

I had a most amazing dream. I was sitting at a massive table, seating twelve of the archetypes. These twelve told me they represented the archetypal signature, as twelve has meaning above and below...twelve Apostles, twelve hours of day and night, and so on.

They assured me that there are indeed other Archetypes. New ones are presented as times and humanity changes. But the basic ones represent the building blocks of human experience. That's Saturn and Capricorn for all you astrology folks. It appears that these twelve were the primary ones. Who knows. But my dreamscape played into that. There are primary ones and individual ones as well as probable archetypes, these twelve said.

Here's how they explained it. The Arch archetype is the head dude. It is non-entity specific in that it has neither gender nor personal identity. It serves as a causeway to the infinite. It also reflects both ways to the infinite and down to the twelve archetypes. It is non-changing and eternal.

The twelve primary archetypes are holding stations for energies required on Earth. These energies weave the very fabric of dimensional existence. They are grounding rods for experience and focal points for the process known as change. We are always under their guidance and protective aura.

We live through each day, usually unconscious of their effects upon us but subconsciously aware of the interplay between them and our choices. Archetypes interconnect with the twelve as we adapt them to our own lives. The individual archetypes are our own personality and our ego.

Ego is not a bad thing but a tool to move the energies around. Ego is very young, positive energy. The altered ego is the screaming two-year-old in the thirty-year-old's body demanding attention.

Individual archetypes change throughout our lives. Probable archetypes are potential yet grounded in corporate reality. These are the doorways to the future; they change as well as we change. The twelve primary archetypes present themselves to us as we journey through life. We seem to have favorite archetypes that blend well with individual personality, and actually, there are new archetypes being born all of the time as humanity progresses.

These archetypes keep coming up in our life, and we do connect with all twelve, though at different times during our life. After the archetypes at the table were explained to me, they all went around the table and told me their job description.

The Fool started. The Fool said, "I'm playful, but when I'm negative, I just waste everything."

The Sage said, "I'll give you wisdom, but you have to ask for it. My negative is I hold things back."

The Magician said, "I transmute everything, and I can help you create reality. The negative is I just forget who I am."

The Ruler archetype said, "I overcome all things, but my negative if I go there with you is I'll just get rid of everything before you can even see it."

The Creator archetype said, "I connect you with everything, and if I go negative, I cut you down, and I criticize you."

The Destroyer said, "I'll give you opportunities, but if I'm negative, I'll ruin them before you can even find them."

The Innocent archetype said, "I asked for help, and I give you this ability for you to ask. But if I go negative, I am the victim, playing out the victim abuser."

The Orphan archetype said, "I set boundaries with things. I will help you in your recovery process, but if you don't call on me, I will sabotage you."

The Warrior archetype said, "I prepare change. I prepare the path, and I give you the fire that you need. If you won't accept the fire in a positive way, I'll destroy everything in your path."

The Caregiver archetype protects, and if we don't use it positively, it will smother and codependently try to nurture what doesn't need to be nurtured.

The Seeker archetype said, "I let everything happen. I'll just be allowing and if you don't seek me out, I'll just get lost in you I won't let you find your way."

And the last one, the Lover archetype said, "I passion for everything, and I connect everything, and if you don't connect with me positively, I will just deny that that even happened."

The twelve archetypes went on to say that when we are our best and worst selves, we are acting under either the positive or negative poles of one of the archetypes. We can be under the influence of one or more. I then asked them why we currently connect the Middle Ages, like Camelot and King Arthur, to so many of our archetypes. They said that there are numerous so-called open pathways to that time available to us. The magic and mysterious beauty we attach to it are similar in energy to the archetypes themselves. And then I brought up the issue of there being four archetypes we all share and others that are individual, making up twelve.

> *The twelve archetypes went on to say that when we are our best and worst selves, we are acting under either the positive or negative poles of one of the archetypes. We can be under the influence of one or more.*

Is that like a zodiac? I heard one woman's version of this and wondered if it was true. The archetype said that's true but only for that person and for those who adhere to her beliefs. Just like this explanation is an entire reality unto itself, so is hers, and so is anyone's for that matter. In truth, archetypes are universal. They present themselves in explanatory form for the purpose of our being able to get and use the information. So, I felt that back at the beginning, they reiterated that the archetypes of universal energies were what was true. Energies are perceived as being real and having form when they are available for corporeal utilization.

This dream was so intense. When I awakened, I immediately wrote everything down. I saw the archetypes sitting at the table, and I saw a graph over each of their head, and I had to scribble what they had to say. This was one of the most intense dreams that I've ever had.

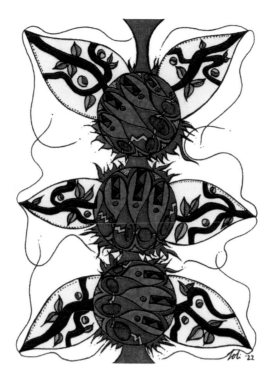

Your Questions Answered:
What are twelve archetypes?

There are more than twelve, and new ones are created all the time. But it appears that in the modern world, everyone seems to have at least one or two of them. There now might be the archetype of the Computer Nerd. But one of the most interesting archetypes that most people seem to have is the Prostitute. That totally freaked me out.

But what it is very interesting. It's not all negative. What if you were a single dad and you had to work? You had three kids, you had to work a job you hated, and you had to lie, then you would be prostituting yourself, but you did it to save your kids. So, we can't just go all black and white with this. All of the archetypes have a negative and a positive node to them, so to speak. And it depends on how we're acting with that.

The archetype of the King, or Queen, is evident. Our egos all want the big, shiny stuff out there. We don't want to be the Prostitute or the Beggar or whatever. But we can be the Beggar archetype. Sometimes, we just need to beg; we need to be the victim. We're playing all these roles.

Along those lines, I had an interesting epiphany last week: my emotions drive me crazy. And I wonder, why can't I get ahold of this? I got a very clear image that the emotions are what make us human. Emotions are the backbone. I don't think emotions are an archetype, but they feed into every archetype because that is how we enact them. That's how we connect with them. We can connect to it mentally or spiritually, but when we connect to it emotionally, it appears to be involved in relationships. I'm getting more comfortable with that, too, with my Cancer Moon, Cancer South Node, all this Cancer and stuff that I've got and the Pisces and stuff, which is very emotional.

That is why we feel so deeply. So, the real catch with the archetypes is how do we take the archetypes and discern how they fit into our lives on a daily, yearly, and lifetime basis. Some of them we have for a lifetime. And some of them come and go. They're like roles that are almost like the astrology chart. Certain planets come in and out. And we will be asked to play roles in this life. And that is what the archetypes are. They're the players on the stage.

There are some wonderful archetype cards. Carolyn Myss has some that are like role cards that go into inner psychological work. There are also websites about the archetypes. It can be extremely confusing because there are a lot of different opinions on it, and they don't agree. But welcome to Earth.

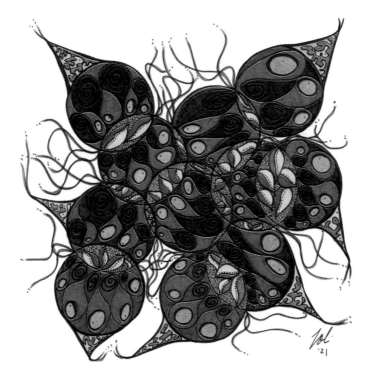

Your Questions Answered: How can people draw out the positive attributes of each archetype rather than dwelling on the negative?

We can't. We're just people. We're just dumb, so we just can't help ourselves. That's what's funny about it because we can see other people doing it, but we don't want to do it. We don't want to get caught. If you could look at the archetypes as the players on the stage and we interact with them.

We're going to get the negative and the positive. I might say, "Oh my God, I'm doing so well with this, and this is a positive aspect." Boom. In ten minutes, here comes the negative piece because I've attached it to something in the past, or I've lost confidence, or I've done something dumb. What we're looking for is how to feel without emoting negatively. Feelings and emotions can be the same thing. But how do we feel that deeply? We also have the engagement of all the neurotransmitters. We want to feel good.

It's that dopamine, give me a big piece of chocolate feeling we seek. We want the serotonin; we want to sleep well. So, we are always seeking the better, and that's what life is. We should seek that. But then we beat ourselves up when we can't do it all the time, and that also is just human nature.

I fight myself with this. It's just ridiculous. If you look at my astrology chart, I almost have what's called a natural chart. I was born on April 10th. I have Mars in the first house. So, I kind of follow the seasons. And I think I'm a lab rat for the universe to try this stuff out on.

Maybe everybody is. When I look in the mirror, I see me. That's the only one I see. Right now, I'm driving myself nuts. I have maybe fifteen girlfriends and probably twelve of them are single. I have just had it with this thing about the boyfriends. What I'm hearing now, and I don't know if this is an astrological thing, it may be an archetype thing: They meet this guy, he's all great, and they tell me about him, and then the next week or two weeks, he's an asshole. And it's this cycle of over and over and over. So, I've had to tell a couple of them that I can't hear about their life like that. They smile and call me a judgmental asshole. I smile back in agreement.

When we tap into an archetype of ourselves that we haven't looked at before, we're going to see honesty. And what I'm having to say is, it's not healthy for me to hear this up and down because I know what's coming next week.

I need more married girlfriends who understand that marriage is hard, but you get along, and you fix it. You stay in it. It's the wonderful parts and the asshole parts that make our lives.

zoliartexoticamontana.com/music

Tatanka Nazin's Walking Song

C'hin Lao:
No such Thing as Supposed To

Here is an article I channeled around 1990, from the amazingly cool astral being calling himself C'hin Lao. In order for energy to manifest on this plane it is necessary for human beings to take action. There is no such thing as supposed to. We often hear you resign yourselves to fate by giving away your power to some pie-in-the-sky ideal called supposed to. What actually occurs when human beings make choices is that the probabilities come either closer to the level of manifestation or move further away from it. What you feel as the supposed to is the probable future which is closest to the surface of your conscious recognition of the event.

When you allow energy to flow freely to you, the greatest good will level out closer to that surface point. Alas, what is the difference between supposed to happen and allowing the greatest good to come forth without undue stress? Focus. When you focus on a particular outcome, you are giving your own God power to a probable future. This is your conscious choice. Do you keep your power centered and focus it on a desired outcome? This focus will energize the probability of allowing what you desire to gather atomic structuring for manifestation.

On the other hand, if you say, oh, whatever happens is supposed to, you play the part of being the victim of circumstance. This means you do not use your focus to choose among the possible outcomes but become a pawn in the game of fate. Allowing us to define fate as that which occurs if you take no conscious action to maintain your focus on a desired outcome defines your astrology chart, your numerology chart and other divination things set in motion at the time of your birth, which will take over when you are unconscious making unconscious choices.

> *Oft times, you feel powerless because you are focusing on only one option. When you find yourself in a hopeless situation, ask yourself why you see only one door.*

So, what have you learned? Perhaps the ball is back in your court. Our purpose is to remind you that you have a say in the choices of your life. Are problems and issues not a request that you choose, but choose which path to take? Are relationships not a daily scenario of probable paths, choices to agree with or disagree with using your own free will? Surely, all life is choice. We say unto you that you have power to retain your sense of self-worth.

You have options to choose. Even in the world of spirit, there are options presented. We choose, we focus. It is, you see, not something you can avoid. The illusions of your dimension, however, create voids and vacuums in this process. Oft times, you feel powerless because you are focusing on only one option. When you find yourself in a hopeless situation, ask yourself why you see only one door.

You will find that the subconscious mind has circled your conscious-recognizing mind with a veil. This veil is a gift from the subconscious, from the past which then invites you to see where you have blocked yourself. Process the issue and watch the other doors appear as the veil lifts. So, you have choices, you have hope, always. Never lose hope. You do have the power of your options.

Your Questions Answered: How do you allow energy to flow freely to you?

Well, there's a lot to that. That's a lifelong quest. We have to keep clearing using different techniques and energy work like reiki, body code, emotion code, belief code, and tapping. All of these things clear the messes we get ourself into just by trying to live life.

The first thing that we have to do is to be aware that we don't know everything. We want to know everything and we won't, but what we need to do is clear the pieces of us that don't work, that block us like the big stop signs.

Once those start getting cleared, it rolls over into being a better magnetic force because everything is electromagnetic in material worlds and even in gaseous worlds. We have to become better magnets for so-called spiritual things. And what we mean when we say something spiritual it is something that gets us off the Earth.

I had a very peculiar experience simply sitting in my chair looking out the window, and I thought, what is this? Earth is solid, and then there's gas, and rain comes into all of it. That kind of realization led me to understanding something I can't even define right now.

And I'm very big on saying follow the prompts. Just be curious and follow what you think that little thing is tickling the back of you. What is that? Be curious about it and ask for help from spirit. Ask to know more about the steps you need to take to become a better mediator and channel of these energies, and a better person altogether, one who is all burning our karma.

Not everything is karma, but it will become so. Not everybody who has a good or bad relationship knew each other in past lives. It's more common that that does happen. But anytime that we engage in anything, we create equal and opposite reactions. And that is the kind of thing that will allow energy to flow through us.

We mess up all the time. We're in an absolute thick energy field; our soul is way beyond that and it's perfect. It's a master on its own plane. And the purpose of becoming more of an energetic magnet for good things is to allow the soul to come through more and more and more. And when that does, we will want to serve, and we will want prayer meditation. We want a way of being that is calm inside but able to act in the physical plane. Because if we can't use this out there, what's the good? Everything becomes self-centered and narcissistic.

Constantly wanting to grow and change, that's fine, but did you brush your teeth today? Did you check your bank account? How are your relationships? All of that stuff is not always first, but it has to be coincidental.

We have to take care of this physical vehicle that we're in. It can be easy to forget that. And a lot of spiritual practices do forget that. No matter what, we still have to come back to physical in this world.

A lot of times, that forgetting is on purpose, to detract from the desires of the body. All these wants that we have are the desires to control our lives. So, fasting can be good. Though, I don't think beating yourself in the back with a stick to get spiritual is good. That's the old Piscean way of suffering, but every age will have a way.

What continually comes up is the idea of prayer, fasting, and meditation. To deny the body the demands, listen to what you are demanding and consider what you are feeling as a need is actually just a want.

Can I do that? Sometimes I can. I went through a period where a spirit shared that it was time for me to experience and know about fasting. I went through a period where I did intermittent fasting, and I was eating only small amounts of food.

It made me clearer, but I was hungry all the time, and that's very distracting. Life is a school full of all these classes. The desires of the body are part of that. We have hunger, which is also an emotional desire. My therapist says food is never an addiction, neither is sleep. Or you can be addicted to eating fat, but that's not a food addiction because those things are needs, they're not wants.

I'm amazed with myself after the fasting thing. It felt great, and I thought I would always continue. Well, a week later, forget it. I was back pounding sugar. It feels like all of a sudden, the energy field disappears and we're no longer able to easily navigate that class. It's like we've gone outside, and the classroom is locked.

When we go into the dream world, many times we have those classes and we bring those back here. It's all interconnected. And that can help the energy shift.

The astral world, the dream world, and what we call our world here really do interconnect. You just can't separate them. We feel like they're separate because of where our consciousness is. We don't all have this continuity of consciousness.

Your Questions Answered:
Why do some people tend to seem like they get stuck in a place?

This has happened to all of us at some point. I don't mean being stuck in a place where you're living for years and years, but everyone has had that experience of trying to get out of a situation that just wasn't feeding them anymore. Sometimes it's a third chakra lesson of learning how to endure without changing to an easier way of being You just have to live in it and you have to do your work, and you will grow. Sometimes it's that situation.

Other times, we are not employing every morsel of guidance available. We're multi-dimensional. But mainly human beings, I think we're lazy. When we don't accept help and act the fool, we're too comfortable with the habitual dysfunction. It's just it's just human nature.

We'd rather stay with what we know. The unknown is fear, and it means that you're out of your zone. I was joking with a friend of mine the other day, who was moving to Los Angeles from the East Coast. And I said, look, if this was back in the pioneer days, even before that, if you did that trip you'd never go back again. You're not going back to Boston when you are down in Sacramento. But as it is now, we have these choices as the world speeds up, as things speed up.

I don't think there's a pat answer for much of anything. A lot of those answers will change with the different times that we're in. But to get stuck in one place, I certainly felt that when I moved here from the farm. I was brought here to be with my husband, to live in Montana, to do all this work I do that I could not do if I were still running a farm. There is no way. I wouldn't have the time.

It's never perfect. Damn it. We just want it to be perfect. We're just insatiable. This is why we keep coming back and saying, "Oh, I could have done that better." Yeah, I could have, but is it worth going through another lifetime with somebody you don't like to try to get it better? No. But we're dumb. We just keep doing it.

So, as we evolve or shift, we become less dumb. We evolved from our past ourselves. Now, we should become somebody we don't even recognize. I am clearly not that person anymore as I was when I was in sixth grade. I can remember the dumb stuff that I did with my friends, but I'm not that person. I still have the memories of that person. We want to evolve out of the unauthentic programmed self of habitual misery. We evolve to become the soul-inspired us. We aspire to become more of who we really are.

Things become less dramatic, and they're more even, so we don't flip as fast from one end to the next. We tend to take things more as they come and keep ourselves out of stupid situations because we've removed the magnetic imprints that attract these things to us and us to them.

Everything's about the magnetism. I was listening to a checker at the food store the other day go on and on about her personal issue of what bothered her about a certain kind of person.

And I wanted to say, "Sweetie, you know, that attitude right there is what keeps those people in your life." Is she stuck? Yeah, but I've been just as stuck. I went through a twenty-year recovery process for co-dependency, making one dumb choice after the next. But that is what I came here to do, and I came here to learn that. Once you learn something, you can teach it. Hopefully, just by being who you are and demonstrating what you learn through kindness and through being able to be in a hard room to read.

What I mean by that is we've got to be able to have a back bone strong enough, who are courageous enough to be able to stand these trials and not run away from them. And sometimes that's staying in a place that you don't like.

Certainly, there are economic reasons why I'm living in Montana. We're a poor state. But if you look at what's happening with housing all over, but especially in Montana, we have a very large young workforce, and there's no place for them to live. So, we're a whole community of apartments. There are thousands of apartments here, more than houses, because we don't have the land or it's not available to be built on. So, as things change, we get stuck in certain situations, but we forget that things will change. Sometimes I would whine, "Oh my. I'm so landlocked here. There's no ocean in Montana." Well, clearly there's not. I've always lived close to the ocean. And Spirit said to me, "Zoli, it is not over yet, for God's sake."

As we evolve, we take things more into perspective, and we're more—the favorite word that my Master likes to use that I totally hate because I can't do it— reticent, if I figure that one out, wow. That's part of my life lesson because I'm just not like that. It's like I'm a fourteen-year-old drag queen. I'm just dramatic, but I'm an artist. That's what I do.

This is my thing, as I say to my husband often: life is messy. People are messy, and it's dramatic. Life is very much like that. But as I evolve, my life has become less like that. When I start riling up inside of myself, I have to remember to calm myself down.

There were times that I couldn't. And to me, that is growth for myself.

zoliartexoticamontana.com/music

When I'm Sublime

C'hin Lao:
Dragons Are Not Imaginary

A reader of the Reality Pirate Newsletter asked C'hin Lao to tell him about dragons because he loved the Chinese dragon symbols. There were three specific types of dragons. The K'ur-La were large and yin in their receptive energy. The K'ur-La lived for centuries and had a slow metabolism. They ate very little, but they loved seaweed and sea mammals. They hibernated during certain times of their life. They were silverish pink in color.

During hibernation, they turned very dull, and their skin curled up to allow air into the lower dermal layers. Yes, they could fly. The second kind of dragon was the Gom-Ba. They were reptilian and looked like the Komodo dragon lizard of today. Indeed, they were their ancestors. The

Gom-Ba's diet consisted mainly of plants and vegetation growing near or on the ground. Their wings were vestigial, having devolved from the Kur-La. They spread their kind over warmer areas of the globe.

The Gom-ba did not hibernate because time was beginning to speed up a bit, and the necessity for deep regeneration was replaced by more light coming into the Earth's atmosphere. They had pearlized images on their skin, a mottled and quite beautiful shining color. The third kind of dragon was the Sar-Tahn. They devolved later on into the larger snake species now found in Asia. They swam, were very aggressive, and had wings used as flippers and fins as well as offering them the ability to fly short distances though not as much as the Kur-La, who actually could fly easily.

> *Yes, there were indeed dragons on this Earth. Some now live in other dimensions and will visit you in your dreams if you so desire.*

The Loch Ness Monster is a de-evolution of the Sar-Tahn. They were not vegan and ate much out of the sea. They were green with variations of black and deep purple. They had small horns or some facsimile thereof used as censors. Yes, there were indeed dragons on this Earth. Some now live in other dimensions and will visit you in your dreams if you so desire. The K'ur-La were the wise old souls of ancient Asia. They can be contacted still. Many left on ships and were transported to a planet in the Pleiadian Construct, where they remain to this day.

Your Questions Answered: Do dragons interact with humans?

Not really. It's a fantasy thing. It's something that's in another world. It's likely that in other times and places, they did, but their times have passed, and they go on to higher realms, which is what happened with the dragons. It's happening now with animals who breed in the far north. The polar bear, the Arctic Fox we will have some of them in zoos, but they're scheduled to leave. It also happened with the dinosaurs.

Unfortunately, they're leaving faster than they really should because of our climate problem. Dragons used to be here. Were they physical or were they coming from another world? Once upon a time, they were physical, but we're talking about a million years ago.

They can come into your dreams, but is it real? That's the big thing we don't know. I have two dragon totems, which means those energy fields protect me. I'm very connected to them. Why is that? I don't know. We get very romanticized about things. We're anthropomorphic about things. We want things that we imagined to be here and to be real in the physical world. But if they were, we wouldn't want them because the very allure of having them somewhere else is the mystery.

An Allosaurus might be your favorite animal, but you wouldn't want one for a pet. They're not of the same nature as humans.

One myth says that dragons shape-shifted and became dragonflies. I don't think that is the entire story. Was there an energy transfer? Probably? Part of what the new age community likes to do is to take these wonderful mysteries and say they're all truth. If I think it, then it's real. It's not. It's a mystery. You don't know it's real. You want it to be true, but just because you want it to be true, it doesn't mean it is.

It's like the lady the other day who told me she could bend time. She can change time. No, you can't. There are a lot of people who think that just believing it's true makes it accurate.

That is an abstract ideal, which is in Ray 6. Ray 6 is very good at abstract idealism. The "Go West, young man!" value is how the US started. They had that abstract ideal in their mind and, in a way, we all do that. It's not always bad.

Sometimes, it leads to making great discoveries or inventing something. We have this ideal from somewhere else, and we're wanting to make it real. We dream something up. That's what inventions are about.

There's always this dichotomy with structures. Is it a real structure, or is it something that we've made up? If we can physically interact with it with the five physical senses, we call that real. Dragons are not in that area. They are not real in that way.

We came here to experience life through the sensation of the five physical senses. And that's just that five minutes at the end of the clock. We really do get fooled in that way. But everybody's got intuitive abilities, everybody has psychic abilities, and what we're learning to do now is to integrate those things.

Sometimes, we have to learn things the hard way. Persistence seems to cause pain. We keep going and going. We're trying to get it, but there's something to that grit that creates the pearl in the oyster. It's the very effort of trying and having it being difficult that sets an energy that attracts help and success.

That's why it's important for children, and all of us, to learn persistence. Then, when you fail, don't win, or don't get picked for the team, you don't quit, you stay engaged or you move on in a positive way. Don't wallow, or you'll never grow.

We all get stuck, and that's the point of where we feel failure, where we don't see we're stuck and where we have been before, and we don't see that we can move ahead. I do it. Everybody does it. And that's where that persistence and that hope comes in. That's the little God piece that we want.

Your Questions Answered:
Do dragons live in certain places or are they worldwide?

Dragons are worldwide. They're not physical but interdimensional, in the etheric. They are definitely here as are gargoyles and all kinds of artistic representation.

We have to realize that it's all one field of energy. All of these psychic experiences, the UFOs, the lucid dreaming, all of this stuff is a field of energy, and it all lives in there together. It's like a big soup pot. When I reread that channeling from C'hin Lao, I had forgotten about the water dragon, but it's quite real.

I have not seen one, though I know that they're real. All of these mythological characters are real and valid, but they're not physical. Perhaps, eons ago, they traveled inter dimensionally. I don't know the answer to that.

A lot of fictional portrayals of dragons show they're able to cross realms or dimensions. I wrote in the first book about a time when I was sitting in the living room where we have thirty-foot ceilings. All of a sudden, I looked up and there was a praying mantis that was probably twenty feet tall, smiling, and looking down at me. It scared the crap out of me. And there was a smaller one next to it, just looking and it was curious. I told Thom, "Let me tell you what I just saw."

At the time, I thought it was this nature being. Then, I started reading online that those are aliens. They really do exist, and they come and do these things. So, it was just there checking me out.

I've had so many things like that that happen. I'm not having those experiences right now because I'm very focused on the physical world. I'm not sleeping, and my voice is hoarse. There's something seeking an exit from my inner world to be cognates in my daily life. I awaken in the dark, and all of a sudden, I'm thinking of all these projects. My mind is just going and going and going. Then, my cat will come and sit on me. It's just the times we're in.

zoliartexoticamontana.com/music

The Dolphin Song

Deconstructing Astral Travel

Astral travel can seem convoluted or out there, but we do it all the time. Every time you go to sleep, you astral travel. I mean, every time, that's what you do. Your soul is connected to your body through the silver cord, and you're gone. And that's just one example. Have you ever experienced where you are kind of asleep, and you jerk really hard, and you feel like you're falling?

That's you coming back into your body. Sometimes, people will get a headache while they're not in all the way they have to go back to sleep and get back in their body.

The Monroe Institute specializes in astral travel. They can teach you how to journey out of body, which is the subject of Bob Monroe's book, *Journeys Out of the Body*.

It's nothing I want to do. I have enough trouble staying here as it is. If there was a drug to keep me in the moment, I'd take it.

Astral travel is safe. I mean, we do it all the time anyway. Being conscious when you're astral traveling is a little different. I don't know if that's lucid dreaming. I'm not quite sure. It's not my specialty. It's too much like LSD for me.

The astral world is a different dimension, and it's a universal dimension. Densities are personal. But a universal dimension is a place, or a frequency, or a zone where all people can go and come back from.

> *The astral world is a different dimension, and it's a universal dimension. Densities are personal. But a universal dimension is a place, or a frequency, or a zone where all people can go and come back from.*

The astral world is where you go when you die. You will pass through what is called the Bardo. The karma we live in is called Kama Loca. And if somebody dies from suicide, or if you have an accident or get a disease where you die before your time, you will stay connected to Kama Loca. You will be in the astral realm until the exact time of physical body death assigned, even before your birth. You will remain connected to this Earth life and maybe do some good for others. That's just how it is. And this seems weird, but that is an absolute truth. It's all in Theosophy.

So, is that a realm that's real? Yes, consciousness does live there. And there are many levels, as we've spoken of the astral realm. The first two are just what we call hell. It's like Pluto.

There are seven levels to all of the astral realm. The one above it, the mental realm, and the spiritual realm have seven levels to each, and each one of these is finer than the one below it. It is less dense and is less connected to the physical world that we live in. Where we are now, it doesn't get lower than this. This is it.

You graduate from Earth school, you get a big old star. This is hard. We come here to spiritualize matter, and we do it by being connected to matter. You can't spiritualize matter and be detached from it to the point that you don't connect to it.

You can't live in a state of meditation and not do anything physical. First of all, you just wither away. Second of all, you'll go insane. You may be connected to other things in places, but that's not reality.

Reality is being connected to this physical world, and it's hard. It's not a pretty place. We can have pretty experiences. But in the astral realm, we create those realms in our mind, in our dreams. And so, when you're in the astral realm, there are places that are just of immense beauty. There's nothing more gorgeous than that. That's because the mind has created that. We're creating with our thoughts.

That is one of the first steps, that I was taught when I joined the Rosicrucian Order: to be aware of that. I'm not always aware of it. I mean, that was forty-five years ago, and I'm still not totally aware of that. But here's how thoughts work. People say, if you think something is going to happen, it will. No. If you keep saying yes to that thought as it rolls back around, then it's possible. It's like the clock as it rolls back around to the beginning point again, and that thought comes up again. If you go, no, I didn't really mean that. I don't really think that. Or, what am I thinking? Or yes, that's really important, and I do believe that. Those are the types of thoughts that create. We have to put our willpower and our intent into those thoughts.

That's our will. That's what Billy, Will.I.Am, the Martian was saying when he was standing in my kitchen, watching me while I felt like a lab animal. That's how I felt because I'd never experienced anything like that. But that is what we are headed to in the Capricorn era, the next twenty-five-hundred-year cycle. That is the will. It is using willpower to control the physical world.

Your Questions Answered: Can you get lost in the astral world?

That depends. What part of you are you asking if it would get lost? Because you are in your consciousness, which is in another energy body. Very close to the physical body, there's an energy body, the life form. And then there's the etheric body, where the chakras are. And then you have your astral body. When you die, the physical body, the life body, and the etheric body dissipates, but the astral do not.

People go into the astral realm when they die. Most do, I should say. But as far as getting lost, it can happen if somebody has the misfortune of being in the lower two astral rooms, which are held in what we call hell. That is where all the negativity is on the Earth. It's all stored there, so to speak.

You can get lost in that, but what would happen when you wake up? The astral room is so dreamy and it's so undefined by the rules that we usually go with. If you were to get lost over there, I guess you wouldn't be able to wake up. Is that where people go if they're in a coma, probably? I don't know. It sounds plausible. I know without a body, during near death experiences, people go into the astral realm, and then they come back and they bring the experiences back.

And the question is, what would we lose? Would we lose our ability to navigate? That can happen. That's called a nightmare.

You can lose the connection between your physical and your soul, obviously, that happens when you die. But it cannot happen before you die. If that cord was broken, you would die. And with demonology and with people that are in black witchcraft, that stuff can happen, and it does.

You can't die in your dreams. You can get separated from the silver cord. Something can happen. It's rare, but it can happen. That might be when some people die in this sleep. It would be kind of cool to die in your sleep because you're already there. You don't have to cross over. You're already there.

You can only get lost if you allow yourself to get lost. In that case, you're not really lost; you're on a journey. When I lived at the lake back in Vincent, Alabama, in the 1980s, I used to get in my little Honda Accord, and I would just drive without having an intended destination. I don't know how I ended up back home, but eventually, I'd circle around. I drove all around rural Alabama. I would always say you're never lost. You're just not there yet. And somehow, I always ended up back home. I ended up in Talladega once, at Tuskegee Institute. I also saw old churches and the darndest places; it was a wonderful experience.

I wouldn't do that today, but I did it back then. So, we're only lost if we realize we are. It's very accurate. If you feel lost, you're just in the fog for a moment, and it'll pass.

Your Questions Answered: What is Heaven

The part of the comforting religious idea of heaven that drives me crazy is the belief that when you die, you will live forever in heaven. You won't, but that's okay. It's something that was added to the Christian religion about a thousand years. The only way to get there is to believe in Jesus. Jesus himself said, "You reach the Father through me." But what He meant was that at the first initiation, where you reach more of a heavenly realm, you have to go through Him. He wields the rod of initiation.

You have to go through Him to get there. Levels one and two of the astral levels are what we call hell. They are awful. These levels are filled with all the drama, the evil, the nastiness of humanity, the demonic crap going on, Level three and four are where most people go when they die. So-called dead people hang out there for about two years. Unless it's a suicide, then they're there until their natural time of death. But every person I know who has passed continued some sort of commo with me for about two years after their body death. Then, they're off to greater things.

And you don't want to do a seance and pull them back that's hugely damaging to them. Very damaging. Sometimes they're in a deep sleep. They're in Pralaya. That's the Buddhist word for it. But you don't want to do that.

People have the idea that when their loved one passes, they'll always be watching over them. And then they feel bad that they don't get signs or messages from them. We're all twelve years old. I mean, you're eighty and you think your grandma Mary from the 1700s is visiting you. No. That it is what we want to believe, and love does bring us back. That is very true in the sense that love is always there. And when you get to so-called heaven or when you die, if you expect to see Grandma Mary, somebody loves you enough to take on that role and you will see her, but it won't be her.

People go. They reincarnate. If you expect to see all your dogs, they'll show up, but dogs don't have souls. Animals do not have souls but they do have Spirit. Remember that the invisible etheric sheath surrounding the body of humans also exists for animals. There are animals in the astral realms, but don't ask me how all that works. There are lots of theories but probably only one truth, which I don't know but I think that it's love. Love is all there really is. Love allows those emotions connected to and with animals to manifest their presence in the heavenly realms. But souls are human only. Sorry.

It's hard for us as humans to consider the bigger aspect of our loved ones, and that the personality we love is only one small aspect of their soul. That's true. We just want what we want. I lived almost my entire adult life looking forward with dread to the day that my father would die. He and I were so close, what a wonderful father he was! My parents were amazing. I adored him. And when he finally did, my life changed. That's what I was intuiting that my that my life would change. I would "adult." And I did meet him a couple times on the other side. He was a delightful guy. But after two years of commo, he went on to other realms.

Why people go to the graveside and talk to people is beyond me because you are not there. It's like cracking an egg and throwing the shell away and picking up the shell and talking to it. The only way to get rid of a body healthfully is to burn it. And you want to wait three days for the other finer bodies to level out and dissipate. That takes three days.

We have a permanent atom called the seed atom which was present when we were created. It is found in each body we have ever had. The seed atom is found in the right-hand etheric heart. That heart is, like all other aspects of our physical body, an act replica of what we call our heart. The seed atom is the only eternal piece we have. It contains the record of all lifetimes, thoughts, actions, memories, etc. It is eternal and does not dissolve or end. But the reason why we have awful diseases continue to plague us is due to our fault of burying bodies, especially diseased ones. Syphilis, Cancer, and Tuberculosis are endemic in the soil. Animals eat the vegetation; we eat the animals as well as the produce.

As humans, we spend so much time taking our dead and putting them in a box in the ground, and then going back there and lovingly placing mementos on the graves. It seems like a form of worship. It is grieving. And I have great compassion for it. There is love there. We just want to still touch them. We just want them to be there. We're all still like children in many ways. We want Grandpa to still be there for us because we love him.

And it's just part of understanding human nature. It's sad. Grief is when we're closest to God. There are some fascinating traditions around death and grief. I like what the Zoroastrians do. They take the bodies up on top of the mountain to dismember it and feed it to the vultures and eagles.

That's what I told Thom he should do with my body. He's like, "Yeah, I don't think that's going to happen." But we're attached to these things. We spend all these years going through all this stuff. We want it to have value. So, we bury it and put it in this expensive tomb and it's just ridiculous. It's ridiculous what we do. But we bury diseases like syphilis, tuberculosis and cancer. Those are the three. We say, "Well, it's dead. It doesn't go anywhere." Well, energy created is never destroyed.

We're on the Earth and we are hurting things. Then, our food and water flow through the Earth. So, how could it not affect it? It's pretty bad. If you leave a dead body in a warm room for two days, you're not going to think it's so great. Embalming became fashionable here during the Civil War because there had to be some way to get the bodies back. There were so many people who died, away from home. Egyptians had it down, though they had some weird rules too. We're all weird.

We're not even close to knowing all the answers. I can pontificate about it all that I want. But when will we really know? Perhaps when we're out of these dense animal bodies and onto better things, but who knows? By then, who cares? Hopefully, you're off to planning your next adventure, your next life, because you live forever. You never quit living in one form or another. Your created soul is eternal, I promise. You'll go from one form of energy into another until who knows when. Because you live forever, but not in the same old tired sick animal body that we call us. We never quit spending time with those who love us, not necessarily deceased family and friends, but so many souls out of body, see? How reassuring it would be if we could see that all the time.

You're either in a physical body or an etheric one. We are truly just energy, plain and simple. That pure energy drops frequency to become physical, like objects, bodies, nature, etc. That pure energy is who you are. You were created as that, and as energy you remain, despite the density of physical forms inhabited in numerous incarnations. That's what makes people afraid.

We die and that's it? No, but our personality identifies with the dense body, thinking, "That's me, that is who and all I am." One of the biggest shocks is waking up on the other side, so to speak. This is especially true for folks who have had the tragedy of dementia, being comatose, or whatever, and their body dies. Then, all of a sudden, they're awake, again.

That would take some getting used to and we get plenty of time to do it. We're never truly alone, you know this. Perhaps we are required to play that silly game to seek the Creative Higher Power. We're always surrounded all the time with those who love us, not necessarily deceased family and friends, but so many souls out of body, see? How reassuring it would be if we could see that all the time.

There are around 60 billion souls available for Earth incarnation. Think about that. What an honor it is to be here. Don't waste it. We have over 8 billion souls on the planet right now, but it holds only 4 to 4.5 billion in a balanced way. We're overpopulating the Earth, you think? But we're here to feel life.

And then if you can't feel it, you can't change it. We can't get along. It's crazy to me. It seems like even in the last five or ten years, how much more divided people have been. The community aspect of things seems like it's diminishing. It will cycle back around for sure. These are the times and the changes. It will all come back around, but it takes time. Everything has to break down in the Ray 1 energy; the ray of destruction. It has to break down as it gets rid of the old over and over and over again.

Do you know what a dermestid beetle is? Talk about a Ray 1 animal. A vulture is also a Ray 1 animal because it eats the dead. It gets rid of things. If I had a basement that I didn't care how it smelled and a huge fish tank, I would fill it with dermestid beetles, wood bark, and a dead deer head. Those dermestid beetles will strip it clean down to the bone. They will deflesh that deer, and it is the coolest thing that you've ever seen.

I wanted some as pets until I went into our tanner and he asked me if I wanted to see how they smell. When you walk into the back area where they keep them, your eyes will water. You will see how they smell, and it's just rotting flesh. But the dermestid beetle is to me a symbol. It should have been like the scarab; it should be everywhere that we have to eat the past to create the future. This is a typical Zoli thing. We have to eat the past and poop it out just to be able to flush it away. Otherwise, it overstays its time and rots.

zoliartexoticamontana.com/music

Lay Me Down

Going Within

The astral world and dreams are very private. We have other people in our dreams, other people that we meet in the astral realm, but it's really a private going within. It's almost a meditative feeling. But what I want people to get out of it is to do this work for yourself. This is my work. This is what I do and I'm telling you how I do it, but I'm hoping that it's going to trigger people to ask questions and to look within themselves.

Dreams are very personal. They really are. Just sit here and think about that. It's kind of a silent journey. And what I'm practicing, or working towards practicing, what I'm trying to do is to learn how to stay conscious while I am dreaming. This is called the continuity of consciousness. And I can't do that yet, but there are people who can. The Masters of Wisdom reveal that it will release our fear of that unknown space between the waking and dreaming worlds. When we can retain lessons from our dreams while awake instead of having all that precious cargo filter down during the day. It will be infinitely clearer

And if I can do that, if I can go into my dreams and say, oh, I'm dreaming, and get comfortable in that landscape, I can bring back much more information where it doesn't have to filter down during the day. It'll be clearer. They say that it releases fear because we are not afraid of the dream or the nightmares or the other worlds because they're two very separate worlds right now to us; our waking state and the dreaming state.

Sometimes I wonder if I'm aware at all in the waking state. Sometimes we live in a daydream state of mind. Daydreams occur when we are in a different density, a collected space of energy unto us only. We are somewhere else; you know what I mean. Our consciousness is not totally focused in the physical world. Like if somebody goes, "Hello, where were you?"

And you think, "Oh, I'm back." But where was I? So, that's a different state of consciousness, and we seem to flip in and out of it a lot during the day. And it's almost like we take a little break. We take a little rest from attenuating to physical consciousness in a way that the mind, body and spirit interact. We pop in and out of it during the day, and I think creative people do that a lot. And I count myself as one of those people.

It's a really funny feeling. If you're driving and you're just kind of daydreaming, then you realize you weren't paying attention and you think, where was I? You don't remember driving the route that got you to where you ended up. I wonder what autonomic system is driving my truck for me?

We take it to be a very natural thing. So, we have that state also. We can probably experience realities with other groups. I know we can with other people too. I recall a way cool experience from fifty years ago. A buddy and I had crashed on the floor watching TV and fell into a dreamy state of being. We both experienced the same density as if we were in another world together. We chatted as we observed the dreamy landscape. I don't recall how long he and I were there but it was truly magical. We were both mediumistic and creative enough to have either created or accepted as a gift this sharing of another world. Have you ever had anything like that happen? I know some of you have.

We could see it and we were talking about it. It was crazy. I've never had that happen again. But I think that kid was very mediumistic also. There's anything out there that you can imagine. What is out there and what's in here? We try to make sense of it, and we try to be conscious of it.

We aspire to communicate how we ourselves experience what may be vastly different from someone else's experience of the same event. We use words. We use pictures. I love doing that with other people, listening to others' intriguing experiences. But hey, you don't need me to say it's okay or that it's real. You don't need me to confirm that. That is YOUR reality, so enjoy it.

When we grow in our awareness of things other than the physical, we can create greater understanding and put fear to rest among us. The words, images, visuals...these are the stuff of theatre and movies. These images from consciousness are played out on the human stage. Think about what it takes to create and assemble all of those parts. We're literally recreating reality and inviting others into our creation. How cool is that?

That's why no two people sleep the same way or experience things the same way. We want to bring other people into our world, and other people want to bring us into their world too. And when we do that, when we have a group consciousness, we can really create what are called miracles. When two of us are together, in God's name, we can create these miracles because we're not here to do it alone.

But we have to be willing to do the work. What it comes down to is embracing your unique journey. I would never be able to put everything in this book about the astral realm and dreams. The topic is so vast, there's no way I could put everything in there that I want. I could go on and on and on with it. And we get triggered by other people's personal experiences. So, my goal is not to be strict on this, only to explain it and to be real. And I don't wander around during the day thinking about this stuff all the time.

I'm a Montana housewife. I will always say that very distinctly. That's how I identify. Regularly, I just think about so-called normal things. And these other abnormal things filter in and out of my mind and my consciousness. Is it more than other people? I don't know. I have no idea.

Don't we all have a personal definition of normal we do try to fit into varying degrees? As we age, we may understand the value of a reticent and perhaps reluctant acceptance of societal laws and values. Or maybe not. You choose. But this is diversity and the beauty of free will, no? I put a lot of thought into this a while back because I got so tired of feeling I wasn't normal or that I was old and these other people weren't normal. There was a time when I felt like I was so abnormal I must be an alien. Fortunately, I got clear guidance that, no, you're not, Zoli.

> *We want to bring other people into our world, and other people want to bring you into their world too. And when we do that, when we have a group consciousness, we can really create what are called miracles.*

But it's normal to have an appropriate reaction and response to the stimuli of the space and time that you live in. In other words, how we react and respond now might be normal, but a hundred years from now, our normal may be considered psychotic.

As the Italian saying goes, . That encourages us to try to be abnormal in a normal world and appear at least to fit into an abnormal situation. We all have a need to belong in some way. Then we have to find some sort of medium to work in. There's kindness and compassion involved in that also. We want to communicate with other people. We want to understand what people are saying. We don't have to agree with them, but we want to live gracefully in a world that really doesn't have much grace, and it's up to us to do that.

The astral world and dreams are all about emotion and our effort to normalize that reality on a peculiarly unfamiliar playing field. We're just trying to figure it out. When we spend time in those spaces, we can bring that into our daily lives, that's just pure creativity.

And if only that was a skill we could just turn on and off. If we work at it, we might get there. I joke and say, I don't drink. I don't do drugs. Nothing. If there was a drug to teach me how to be here present all the time, I'd take that. Be here now. I'd be hooked because I don't know how. I'm an emotional wreck most of the time.

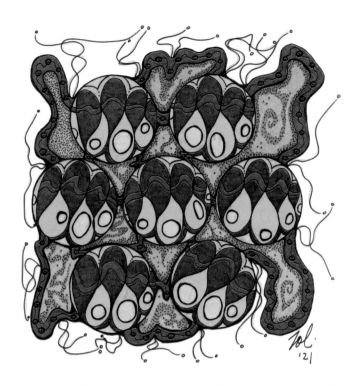

Your Questions Answered: How does the Moon and emotions play into the astral world and dreams?

In our astrology chart, our Moon represents our emotions. And wherever our Moon is in the chart, it has to be satiated. For example, my Moon is in Cancer. I am a homebody. You cannot get me out of this house. It is what I love to do. I'm good at it, and I love it, and I'm emotional. So, my Moon is actually in the natural house of Cancer, so that helps. But if my Moon were in Capricorn, I would want to be out in the business world. I would feel more emotionally satiated if I were a businesswoman.

So that is one aspect, but how does that relate to, the astral world and dreams? I theorize (and that's an important word to use here) that our Moon placement in our astrology chart will determine much of our experience in the astral realm. Because that's where we go.

Our emotions flow through our dreams. And the emotions have got to be taken care of. They have to be nurtured. So, if the Moon and the astral realm are intricately connected, that would make sense why the Moon is called the enchantress.

The Masters say that the moon is a dead satellite, and in the distant future, they're just going to haul it away and get rid of it. I don't know how that's going to work with the tides, but the moon influences the waters of the body. Water is in motion. Cancer is ruled by water along with Pisces and Scorpio. But water is fluidity and our body is mainly water.

Our lives have a natural cycle to them. Maybe we dream certain things at certain times, but we don't really realize it. We're supposed to write dreams down the minute we wake up. Some people are good at dream journaling. It makes me crazy. I can't do it unless it's a really, really good dream, and I have had some of those. It's a different world and we're in a different state of consciousness. When we're in the astral world, our consciousness is in the astral body. It's a very real thing.

We have shifted. It is like all fingers pointing to the astral realm. When you wake up, you're not there anymore. You're in the physical world. So, why would we remember all that? You can practice that and get better at it. And even at age seventy, I want to work at that. But I think that's why you forget. You're in a different world.

The Masters say we can develop the skill of continuity of consciousness. When you go to sleep, you wake up in the dream, and you can remember this dream. You can act on it. And during the day, when you wake up in the morning, you remember what you did.

It takes time and determination to develop because, once again, we're just dumb. We just don't get it. We're not that evolved.

Being more connected to our dreams is one of the next steps for humanity. There will be a time when everybody does that.

There is a group of Indians in South America called the Suar. They pay attention to their dreams. I wrote a song about it, called "The world is as you dream it." When they get up in the morning and have their first meal, they sit and they discuss their dreams.

That's a very feminine thing to do. It's very intuitive. And what is happening now is men are much more able and given social permission to access intuition and feelings. That is what the feminine energy is. Being in touch with the feminine allows for being more in touch with the astral.

Your Questions Answered: What do you think about the idea of a 5D world?

Like everything else in spiritual dogma, it is half true and half bullshit. We're always trying to escape. We're always trying to get away from difficulty or pain.

What I understand the 5D to be, is the next step. You can be in the fifth dimension while you live in the third dimension. The third dimension, of course, is the physical. The fourth dimension is movement and time. And the fifth dimension is when you're in the astral, or etheric.

The fifth dimension is extra-physical and it is where all this new technology and these new ways of being are. I've had experiences that I know were fifth dimensional because I was out of time and space. I can't explain it because I've never had that experience before.

I was watching things happen around me and it felt like I was just not there. I was physically there, but I was not there. But wait I was there because I was conscious of my existence. I was going through all of these things in my head.

This is something that we're getting into, and more and more people are going to be able to access it. A lot of people act like 5D is a set place, almost like the rapture that Christians of some denominations believe. People will experience more of an evolution, rather than a departure. What's important to remember about it is that if you're here in your body, you have to finish it.

You do not get to escape into some other dimension You can do all kinds of weird drugs, get drunk, and smoke yourself into oblivion, but you're going to come back into it and wonder what happened. The fifth dimension is being even more conscious, in an extrasensory way.

We are not entirely spiritual. We have to be here. We have to be physical. We don't have to be earthy, but we do have to have a mental attitude towards spiritual things. Because if we just go with the astral/ emotional, we end up chanting for fifteen hours, and thinking that we're going to ascend.

And you're not. Clearly. You'll ascend to the top of the bureau in a vase with your ashes. That's it. I can be kind of rude but I'm just trying to keep things kind of basic.

I'm a basic person. My birth father was an engineer. My birth mother was a cashier at a grocery store. I don't come from great erudite, aristocracy. I just want people to be kind to each other. Just be basic and quit trying to act smart. Just be yourself.

In my experience, when I do that, I'm fine. When I get threatened by people and I start using quarter words in a ten-cent conversation, I sound like a freaking idiot and they know it.

One thing a lot of people need to hear is that you get to be yourself. You don't have to live up to these aspirational astral and spiritual states of being. It's all part of who we already are. You don't need a big spiritual leader to take you there. It's right there.

Religion is only one way to access God, to access spirit. Those are called devotional energies. There are times when I'm in devotional energies, and I'll go to mass, I'll be praying more and reading more about that. Then, it's gone and I'm accessing God through nature, or through my writing, or through communication with people. God is everywhere. We're taught to believe that the only way to access it is through devotional energies and that's not true.

We get scared when we can't figure things out and we run to the authority figure, either in our mind or visiting an educator, a priest, a guru; somebody that we think knows more. Maybe they do, but we have to figure it out on our own sooner or later. And unfortunately, you have to do that by yourself. That's always around Ray 1, the ray of destruction, and it's very misunderstood.

I've already written some on this topic, but it's very important to realize that every millisecond of the day, something is dying or leaving. And there is a new piece coming in. It's a constant renewal and resurgence, but something has to go for something else to come in. And we have to grieve that sometimes. We have to grieve the loss of friendships, relationships, our age, we grieve these things and sometimes when we don't want to do that, we get all locked up with drugs and alcohol, excessive this, excessive that, and hopefully we get out of it.

But it's all part of this path of just constantly renewing over and over again. The things that we don't want to end are all the dopamine receptor things. All the fun things, all the good things. We don't want that to end.

We are here to be human with all the warts and faults and mistakes we make, we're here just to be people. At times, I have a lot of trouble with that. I'm highly judgmental myself because I'm so insecure. Emotionally, I think I should get everything and when I don't, I beat myself up. And we all do that at times. We tie ourselves into knots about it. Welcome to Earth.

zoliartexoticamontana.com/music

Echoes Of the Mesa

Conclusion

All go into the astral world when dreaming, but may visit different layers depending on what one believes and how one behaves in this dense physical waking world. Our daily world has only one level, waking consciousness, but the seven levels of the astral etheric attract people according to their degrees of so called evil or good. Like attracts like magnetically and acts out electrically. All earthly habits and beliefs are acted out in the dream states and are extremely intensified in the Astral world.

All appear in a body reflecting what their thoughts would look like. Mean people will appear, well, you get it. Those people living life in addiction, their desire body, placing sensation (sexuality, food, drink, glamour) above their ability to control those emotional desires, will likely experience that in the lower astral levels.

Level one and the lower part of level two are dense, what we label as hell. It is as real as one imagines it to be and will be experienced as earthy thoughts. The upper level of two and astral level three are somewhat less dense but are still enamored with energies from and of the earthly life. Most undeveloped souls go to level three at death if they are simply ignorant rather than consciously choosing evil. Levels four through seven are magnificent indeed, with the higher levels allowing unrestricted beauty, bliss, and heavenly experience. Some souls, after bodily death, may choose to remain there for thousands of earth-time years.

You don't want to receive all of the messages from the astral realm because it's so much glamour and illusion. I'm still trying to figure this all out myself. And I don't know if I'll ever get it because I'm not really friends with the astral realm. I really want more from the mental realm. I want that clarity without the emotional construct added to it. But the dream state is part of that. So, one thing I'm working on is how to be congruent, to be able to go to sleep and wake up in my dream and go, okay, I'm dreaming.

My best advice is that you ask to know why you came here. What did you come here to do? What do you need to work on? And what can you actually accomplish in this life? I totally hate the statement that you can do whatever you want. If you think it, you can do it. That's a lie. Tell Christopher Reeves, who was in a wheelchair, that he could be Superman and fly.

You can't tell people that. The truth is to say, we are supposed to try. We're supposed to put out the effort without knowing if we're going to be able to finish it with the result. We have to be persistent and we have to be consistent and we have to keep trying. And depending on what that is, it could take a lifetime. Find out what you can do in this life. Is it worth it for me to learn three more languages at age seventy so I can talk to people? No.

So, I have to realize I cannot do that. We all have disabilities. We are disabled from doing a hundred percent of everything. And I don't mean just the visible disabilities. For me, mine is autism. I have two hip replacements. I'm old—whatever. So, you modify your life. And how can you modify your life to the changes that happened to you? Take care of your body, the physical body. You might have noticed we get one per life.

We have to take care of the physical. We have to eat right, get some exercise, and get some sleep. And if you can't do those things, get help. Only healthy people ask for help. I always launch back into the recovery movement. I really do the twelve steps in all areas of my life.

That reminds me that we're powerless over things. And that doesn't mean that we're wimps, but to say, look, without the help of the creative energy of God, Buddha, Moses, whatever you want to call it. Without that, we're just a shell. We're a personality. And the personality doesn't last.

When you die, the astral body goes for a couple years, and then poof is gone forever. October twenty-fifth is my mom's birthday. When she died, she stuck around for a couple years. But now she's gone. I'm not going to call her back, but can I take those pieces that I learned from her? Her good advice? And what can I do with that? So, that's where the look for the good and try comes from.

And what can you really do? Everybody needs some sort of counseling at some point in their life. If you don't get it, you're not going to know. We can't always accomplish everything that we get these ideas that we want to do. That's called abstract idealism or magical thinking. I know a lot of people in the New Age community. They drive me crazy, and I certainly drive them to their limits of tolerance. No worries, we're all in this together. With the whole point of it, they're telling me I am part of their community.

I agree that I am part of it, but I'm not going to say if I think it is going to happen, it will come true. That's magical thinking that borderlines on psychosis. You can't just imagine things and then go forward without any practical application. So, I'm very big on the practical.

In the astral world, there's nothing practical about that. That's not even here. So, if we focus on here, right, here, right now, to stay in our body, to try to get things done, and to ask for help from the Beings that Guard and Guide us.

That's my phrase, the Beings that Guard and Guide me. All you need to do is say, "Help me. Where am I? What do I need to do?"

Get practical. Get honest. And listen to what you know the answer to be. And so, I harp on that to get honest. We all try to run away from it. I mean, who wants to face the shit? So, if you can do that in astral travel if you can do that at night when you sleep, it's not taking up any time during the day.

You can go to your job, and you can chop wood and carry water, whatever. And then you can do the astral work at night. I think it would be amazing. I don't think I will ever be focused enough to be able to do it. Maybe when I'm ninety or a hundred, I don't know. I have enough difficulty just staying here, being in my body.

It also depends on what kind of person you are. Are you an earth person? Are you a water person? A fire? An air person? Then, you have all the Ayurvedic doshas. Are you Vata, Pitta, and Kapha? Then, you have Chinese medicine. Are you liver, kidney, or heart based? What is your numerology chart? And the list goes on. What's your astrology chart? I'm very big on finding answers to as much of that as possible because each life is going to be different.

We're focused on this life. How can you use the abilities that you have and the skills that you have taken thousands and thousands of lifetimes if not a million, to come to right here and right now? All of your previous lives led up to this moment. So, if we can take those skills and we can apply them to now, wow, we could change this world.

The show New Amsterdam on Netflix touches on this. It changed my life. I just finished it. It is about socialized medicine and how it really should work, which is what I believe in. But it can't work in the U.S. because our healthcare is wedded to capitalism. Everything's about the almighty dollar. That show demonstrated the ideal of kindness in healthcare of putting the patient before the dollar. Somehow, it will all work out. It showed people who are trying new things. If we aren't afraid to try, and if we just keep pushing and trying in our own particular area, that's how we get things done.

That's truly what it comes down to. So often, we do the same thing that hasn't been working over and over again. And that is the definition of insanity. Yet, we do it until we are sick of it. I'm at this point now in my life that I speak up. I will tell people when I don't want to hear about something. Although we do have to modify our lives, we have to get along with people, we have to have relationships. We have to care about what people think up to a point. We also have to care what we think.

The hardest thing to do in this social media world is, to be honest and authentic. I have a hard time with that. I tell people I'm very insecure, but that's my charm. That's just how and who I am because I'm very sensitive. So, there are certain parts of ourselves that really aren't going to change.

We fight it because we're people. We think we want to change it. Maybe we should. Maybe it's a bad habit. Certain things we can, certain things we can't. The things that we really can't change are other people, other people's choices, or other people's opinions. We can't change that. So, we have to have the dignity and the grace of acceptance and just step away from it, but it's hard.

I like the last part of the acceptance prayer, the courage to change what I can and the wisdom to know the difference. That wisdom is detachment. And Maitreya says that detachment is the greatest drug there is. I had to do that the other day with a girlfriend of mine who had fallen in love with this famous guy. It drove me crazy for two days because I was thinking, "Oh my God, this is going to end badly." I woke up one day and realized all I could do was love her.

That's detachment. It takes work to get there. I've noticed the grief involved in letting go of addictions and demanding, or ranting wants the emotional body to be satiated. When I manage to detach from something, I experience calm. Pacification of desire and a cooling wind blessing the heated emotion I felt was so important.

Emotional detachment is a major life lesson for me. Don't wait up. But we have a process to get there. It's like with your kids; all you can do is love them. You can say or do whatever, but they're going to make their choices. And what is harder than that?

Our marriage counselor says to never stop trying if you think something's important. My mom was great with that. You could not budge her. Patton's army could not have moved her when she really believed something was true. That's a great strength. And there are certain times when we really shouldn't back down. But then we have to leave it alone. That's the detachment. That's the hardest for people who are relentless to be able to find out when they can detach from the situation. And in the astral realm, we find detachment.

What are dreams but an adventure into the silent places of the soul? We have here an opportunity to breathe into daily consciousness a big, fresh breath from the great beyond. Who knows what we may find? Dragons, great landscapes of unearthly beauty, lost pieces from times never known? All is possible in the astral world, yet caution is the best traveling companion. Remember to watch your thoughts because they manifest quickly there. Hold fast to your value system so as not to drop frequency and land in the muck of lower levels.

So, what do you think? Do you feel any differently now after reading this book? I pray you are easy on your learning self and grateful for the hard work you do daily just to stay the course. I love people and have a passion for peacefulness among us. If you can hold onto your values, stay the course and maintain a modicum of humor, I bet you'll do just fine.

Earth school is treacherous and lengthy. We don't always do the best, but we do try. Trying is the fuel of achieving our goal of something better, something more understood, perhaps something sent at the end. I know you have hard times. Don't give up. You never know enough to know the outcome of the shielded lesson!

Don't quit. I promise someone or something will offer you a peek behind the curtain. We have a brilliant future awaiting us. These crazy times presage that. Stay the course. The astral world and your dreams are a birthright to Divinity.

Remember that love is the fuel firing your life both awake and in the astral realm. Love deeply and fiercely that YOU, the divine piece of God, created by Him to illuminate the darkness. You are love, and you are loved. I believe in you. Go in peace!

Zoli Althea

zoliartexoticamontana.com/music

The Great Invocation

Acknowledgements

Thank you to the collaborators who helped in the creation of this book.

Photographic Art:

by Tammy Geneau. Peaceful Simplicity is all about encouragement and enjoying the simplicity that peace brings. I live on the east coast of Canada and I love to photograph God's creation. I use the beauty of nature as the backdrop to bring words of encouragement to a world of turmoil, fear and confusion. It is my hope that in some small way it can make a difference. Please visit www.peacefulsimplicity101.com for more.

Graphic Design:

Tristin is an aspiring artist who enjoyed drawing the Reality Pirate. He was inspired by the artwork he saw in indie games like Hollow Knight and later became interested in character design after playing Banjo-Kazooie. He can be reached at tristindesigns64@gmail.com

Editing:

Linda Beaulieu is an editor and project manager who lives in the forest with her family in Canada. She loves collaborating and helping people share their stories. Contact her at: lindasusanbeaulieu@gmail.com

Formatting:

Trisha Fuentes is a Top-Rated Freelancer on Upwork who offers book formatting and custom book cover design. Contact her at: ardentartistbooks@gmail.com

Request other books in the Reality Pirate Series from your favorite eBook retailer:

The Reality Pirate's Journal: A Thesis on the Nature of Things

The Reality Pirate's Guide to Your Paranormal Normal

Visit ZoliArt for more music, art, and writing:
zoliartexoticamontana.com

Disclaimer

The accuracy and completeness of information provided herein are not guaranteed or offered to produce any results, and the advice and strategies contained herein may not be appropriate for any one particular person or situation. The Owner shall not be liable for any loss incurred as a consequence of the application or use, directly or indirectly, of any information presented in these writings. The Owner is not responsible for the actions or failures of any third parties, nor is the Owner responsible for any advertisements or for any content linked to this book. The Owner makes no representation regarding the reliability of this book. Readers accept all risks. Any claim for damages shall be limited to the amount paid by the claimant to the Owner for services.